Sacrifices
Of A
Hustler

David Simpson

Editor: Katrina Breier

Acknowledgements

I would like to give my thanks to GOD first. Secondly, I would like to thank my kids, Tierra Ervin, Josiah Dixon, Davionna Simpson, and David Simpson Jr., for allowing me to be in their lives, even through my absence. I wanna thank my home boy, Keyjuan Smith, for putting up with me while I was writing this book, I know I got on your nerves. I thank Anthony "Bucky" Fields for inspiring me to write after letting me read a few of his books. And Tommy Slaughter, my boy from Kentucky, I thank you for being a real dude from day one. We went through a lot at Hazelton penitentiary. Also my big brah, Smizz from Philly. I ain't forgot you my dude. Major, Keem, Pelon, Chios, can't forget my main man Jimmy Henchman. You still can't beat me in chess.

I would like to thank my Aunt Renee, Rita, and my lil big sister, Kitabug. Thank y'all for pushing me to continue to write. My sister Ashsa Feamster, for being there my whole bid and not turning your back on me.

Last but not least, Tamiya Merl. We been through a lot and you never turned your back on me, even when I fussed and cussed. You made my bid so much easier. Without you I don't know how I would have made it, besides the grace of GOD.

If I left anyone out I apologize and will mention you in the next one. Thank all my readers in advance. I promise that as you take this journey with me, you will not be disappointed. These books are not real, just thoughts of a man that has seen a lot and done a lot. Until pen meets pad again, ENJOY!

Chapter 1

"I need oxygen in here now...! We're losing him...! Heart rate 61 and dropping...!" The EMT shouted. "More oxygen damn it!"

Those were the last words he heard before he blacked out. Damn! It was all good just a week ago.

"King" AKA, Emory Cummings, was born on June 24, 1981. He grew up on the West side of Salisbury, NC with both of his parents. His mother worked at Rowan Memorial Hospital and his father was a well-known street hustler.

King's uncles would babysit him while his mother was at work. He would sit outside, on the porch whenever he was at home, or wasn't doing homework. His uncles would sit on the porch with him as traffic flowed by. King looked up to his uncles. In his eyes they were real street hustlers and role models. Later on in his life he would find out the difference between the hustler's and those who smoked crack. In other words, "crackheads."

Hustlers on the corner would take turns calling his uncles to make transactions. Chuckie was the older of the two, Len being the younger one. Chuckie would take different amounts of drugs from the corner guys and serve it to customers pulling up in cars or walking by. Before coming back to the porch he would walk down the street to make sure that it was a set-up, the police would get him and not the guys on the corner. King sat and observed this routine daily, it was tantalizing and fascinating to him.

Livingstone College was only a couple of blocks from his house, it was an HBCU school. On Saturdays you could hear the band playing while the football game was going on. Some days Kings' mom would come home tired as a white mouth mule. His uncles would help King with his homework and make sure he showered, then they would all be outside sitting on the porch.

This was a daily routine unless Kings' father would stop by and pick him up. His Father would take him to get something, or out to eat, or just spend time with him. His father, Davion Cummings, or DC as everyone called him, was a well-known hustler that had the city on smash. He had all the cars, women and the money. Everywhere they went people showed respect to DC.

King and his father would normally hang out at the pool hall, on the East Side. The pool hall was only for the hustlers. Everyone who was someone could be found at the pool hall and DC frequented the place quite often. King had witnessed guys lose lots of money to his dad, but his dad had lost lots of money as well.

Seeing his father with all the nice, expensive cars, women, money, and the respect that he had gained intrigued King. Watching his uncles as he sat on the porch, he visualized himself being the best hustler Salisbury had ever seen. King had become a product of his environment. He was 10 years old when he first started selling Candy in school. He would save the Candy that his father and uncles had bought him and would take it to school to sell. He began making a few dollars, $5 to $10 a day at first. He was happy with that.

The teachers started harassing him about selling the Candy and eventually made a phone call informing his mother about his extracurricular activities. Suzanne, his mother, would check his book bag every morning before he left for school. King was well aware of this and the night before he would stash the Candy outside the house. He would then pick it up on the way to the bus stop the following morning.

King was smooth for his age and had recruited his homeboy Satchel to sell the Candy for him in school, for two dollars a day. Suzanne had told her co-workers about King selling Candy in school. They found it hilarious how he thought like his father. She knew the hustler was in his blood.

As King got older, his mother allowed him to go farther from the house. He started going to the local recreation gym, to shoot ball. He had skills for his age. At 12 he started playing AAU for the 12-14 year old group. All of the boys were bigger and more talented than King, but he could hold his own against the older boys. He averaged 10 points, 5 rebounds, and a couple assists a game. He liked balling so much that he tried out for the 8th grade team while he was still in 6th grade.

While playing AAU, which is a league that travels out of town to play different teams, King enhanced his game. He made the game look effortless and he was the youngest of 10 players. Kings' grades were good in school and he was advanced on the court. All the players and coaches respected him and he was well liked. Everything seemed to be looking great for King.

Things took a turn when his uncle got arrested. King had just turned 14 and they were all sitting on the porch as usual. His Uncle Chuckie had handed something to a white man that had pulled up in a Burgundy van. As soon as Chuckie turned to walk away, the police came from everywhere. He was thrown down hard onto the pavement and handcuffed.

His uncle was charged with possession, with intent to sell and deliver. Chuckie's bond was extremely high for just two rocks, $50,000 to be exact. The guy Chuckie was making the sale for didn't even bother to go and bail him out. That didn't set well with DC when King replayed the events to his father. DC and Chuckie were brothers. DC immediately bonded his brother out of jail and Chuckie was on the porch two days later.

The following day King was returning home from basketball practice when he noticed his father's BMW parked on the block. DC was in a very heated discussion with the guys on the corner, particularly Shane, the young hustler Chuckie was running for. As King got closer his father noticed him and lowered his voice. He told King to go in the house and take a shower. King gave his uncle a hug and a pound before going into the house. He knew what the commotion was about, his father was checking Shane for not bailing Chuckie out.

King got into the house and ran upstairs to look out the window. As he watched the men on the corner he saw his father pull a gun so fast you would have thought it was already in his hand. In broad daylight, DC called Chuckie over and had him frisk Shane. Chuckie took money, drugs, and a gun off Shane while his homeboys stood and watched with mean mugs on their faces. No one wanted any trouble with DC.

After taking Shane's belongings, DC told him that he and his crew were no longer needed. DC waved his hand, dismissing the group as they tucked their tales and walked away, defeated.

The next day when Kings' mother came home from work, Chuckie was sitting on the porch counting money. Suzanne stared at him intently, she hadn't seen this side of Chuckie in years.

Looking over her shoulder she noticed that there were no hustlers on the corner. That was a scene that she hadn't ever seen.

"Why do you seem so happy Chuckie?" Suzanne asked.

"Look around you." Chuckie beamed with pride as he swiped his hand through the air. "It's a new day." He stated.

Suzanne turned around looking intently up and down the strip as she played into his scheme.

"I've been given another chance at life. I won't take it for granted again," Chuckie said.

"That's good to hear," she replied.

King stood at the front door laughing at his uncle hysterically.

As the days passed, King noticed his uncle started dressing nicely and he bought a new car. Chuckie also had a woman with him every day. She was fine and younger than his uncle too! As he sat outside with his uncle, King noticed him stash things around the yard. After seeing his uncle's daily routine he started to get curious. It didn't take King long to figure out what it was.

It was a Friday night and King had just returned home from a basketball game. He had taken a shower and was out back hanging with the guys. Chuckie was sitting in his car with one of his many females as King sat on the porch. He had been outside about 30 minutes when out of nowhere, two masked men ran up on Chuckie. They shot him and his companion at close range, letting off about 30 rounds each.

As the gunmen fled the scene King noticed the shoes on one of the assailant's feet, they were the new Huarache's that had just come out. He had seen Shane with the same shoes on earlier as he was getting off the school bus. King waited patiently as the men fled the scene and as soon as they were out of eye sight he ran to his Uncle's car. He wanted to see if he was alive and if there was anything he could do to help.

Chuckie was still breathing, but barley. He was reaching for his cellphone as King approached the car. "I got you Unc," King said, visibly shaken. He grabbed the phone and called 911, then gave the dispatcher the address.

Soon the house was swarming with police and EMT's from the ambulance. Suzanne rushed home and was grateful that King hadn't been hurt. The young lady with Chuckie had died at the scene. Chuckie had been hit in the neck and two of the bullets had punctured his lungs. He fought for his life for the next seven days and then died.

King had gotten the gun and drugs off his uncle before the police had come, although he would never tell his mom or his dad that information. The funeral and wake were both held on the same day, instead of two separate days. King was devastated. He stayed out of school the following week and missed basketball as well.

It had been two weeks since the senseless murder of King's Uncle Chuckie when DC had come to pick King up late one night. Getting out of bed and throwing some clothes on, he went out see what was up with his father

"Where are we going?" King asked his father, still half asleep.

"For a short ride," DC replied with shortness.

They rode in silence for about 30 minutes as the 'Quiet Storm' played on the radio. King had never been this far outside of Salisbury, as the ride continued all he could see was trees and open fields. Finally DC pulled up to this farm that looked as if it had been abandoned for years.

Looking at his father in confusion, King sat quietly, waiting for his father to speak.

"Come on son," DC instructed, finally breaking the silence.

They both exited the car and King noticed a black duffle bag in his dad's hand. He followed his dad towards the abandoned barn. Once they entered the barn, it was pitch black. There weren't any lights on, just candles burning and some light coming through holes that were visible in the barns structure.

As they walked through the different stalls, they came upon two figures sitting in chairs. The men were tied to the chairs with their hands tied behind their backs. Both men were also gagged. King didn't like the sight that was in front of him but before he could see either of the men's features, he noticed that one of the men had on those same Huarache's that the gunmen had on the night his uncle was killed.

King suddenly became dizzy and reached out to grab his father for support. DC glanced at his son and asked what was wrong. All King stated was that he didn't feel good. King had good insight and was an acute observer. DC knew King had already analyzed what was going on.

"This won't take long," DC assured King, putting his hand on his son's shoulder. "Bear with me son." DC knelt and sat the duffle bag on the ground. While kneeling down, he rubbed his chin as if in deep thought. Seconds later he walked over to the men and snatched the cloth off the men's heads.

Sitting there in front of them was Shane and some other guy. King knew Shane but not the other guy. Seeing DC horrified the men and their eyes grew to the size of golf balls.

"I'm only going to ask y'all one question, one time," DC said to the men.

King had never seen this look in his father's eyes before now.

"Don't speak at the same time," he stated as he circled the men like a vulture and then snatched the gags out of both men's mouths.

"Ye... yes... yes sir," the other guy stammered.

Shane just sat there and starred DC straight in the eyes. DC stood front and center of both men and said, "My question to the both of you is why?"

The Uncnown guy was the first to speak, without wasting any time. "It was Shane's idea," he stated, nodding his head in Shane's direction. "He was mad because you ran him and his crew off the block," the guy confessed. "We would ride through the block in different cars and see Chuckie getting money. It made Shane mad," he continued. "But, what really pissed Shane off was when he saw his bitch sitting in the car with Chuckie. She hadn't been home in two weeks." The man was spilling his guts, hoping that it would spare his life.

Shane was sweating profusely, he was beyond pissed off. As the man kept talking, DC knelt down and pulled a gun out of the duffle bag. King looked on, puzzled as his father began to screw something onto the gun. DC stood and raised the gun to eye level in front of the guy. Without hesitation he shot the guy three times in the head. The impact from the slugs knocked the man back with force, knocking him clean out of the chair. DC thought King would turn his head or throw-up, but King stood there, unnerved by what he saw. He didn't flinch or budge, he just sat there staring at DC.

Shane knew he was going to die. Especially after DC heard why they had killed his brother.

"Come here son," DC calmly called King to him. He came obediently and stood beside his father. "In life you will have men smile in your face. You will encounter men that will dislike you and look at you funny for no reason. You will also have men hate you for what you have," DC said, pacing back and forth in front of Shane. "They will be jealous of you for what they don't have." He stopped pacing and looked down at King. "Women have always been a downfall to great men. Hate and pride will always be brothers and sisters and their cousin will always be death!!" DC felt that these jewels needed to be dropped so that King could see niggas and the world for what it was. "Everything I'm telling you is so that you can read between the lies, the deceit, the jealousy, the fake smiles, and handshakes that don't match. These are Laws of the Land. That is why this man killed your uncle, my brother," DC said, smacking Shane with the pistol.

When DC turned around, King noticed that there were tears running down his face. Seeing his father cry made King feel something he had never felt. The feeling was foreign. Without hesitation King reached for the gun and took it out of his father's hand.

DC felt a pair of cold hands touch his own as looked down to see King take the gun from him. DC felt overwhelmed at his son's actions, but once King had the gun he pointed it directly at Shane's head with no remorse. You would have thought that Shane would have begged for his life, but his stare just went from DC to King. As Shane looked King directly in his eyes, King pulled the trigger once, blowing Shane's brains all over the pole that sat behind him.

Chapter 2

After that night in the barn, things went back to normal for King. Ironically, the events of that night didn't bother him much. Even so, DC was concerned about his son after what happened that night. It had been two weeks and he really wanted to talk to Suzanne so he could get a better idea of how King was taking it. They planned to meet at Pizza Hut on West Innes St and both were on time.

Suzanne walked in and DC noticed that she was every bit as fine and sexy as ever. He hated that they couldn't be together because of the lifestyle he chose to live, she never agreed with the line of business that he was in. Most women salivated to be next to DC, but Suzanne always held high morals and principles. That's another thing DC loved about her, he couldn't have her. You know how the saying goes, 'Everybody wants what they can't have.'

Suzanne saw how DC was looking at her and dismissed any attempt of flattery he may be making. She sat down and stated, "Go on and talk. I only have 30 minutes, I can't be late!"

"Always business first," DC replied. "Have some pizza, I ordered your favorite, Hawaiian chicken and pineapple," he said.

She took a slice of pizza as DC started talking.

"How has King been these last couple months?" He asked as he wiped her mouth with his napkin.

"He's been doing good in school and has been active afterwards. He spends a lot of his time at the gym. As far as when he's home, I don't know, you would have to ask your brother. But overall, since Chuckie's death, I think he's coping really well," she said looking at her watch.

"Do y'all talk when you get home from work?" DC questioned, taking a drink of his tea. "Does he seem distant with others?" He continued questioning.

"Yes, after I get off work and home, I ask him how his day was. He also asks how my day was. He's almost never distant, he's a very observant child. I guess he gets that from you," she teased. "DC may I ask you something?" Suzanne had become fidgety.

DC sat up and looked her directly in the eyes as he said, "Sure Suze."

"Well, a couple of my co-workers said that the guys who were responsible for Chuckie's death were found executed in a barn in Woodleaf. It's been all over the news and in the newspapers for the past two weeks. Do you know anything about that?" She quizzed.

"Yes, I've heard about it from the newspapers and he-say she-say stuff." DC lied. "But did I have anything to do with it? No!" He stated firmly.

She had been with him for 15 years and she always knew when he was lying. Instead of pursuing the truth or being lied to, she asked, "Are we finished with this conversation?"

"Yes!" Replied DC.

Suzanne got up and DC stood up as well. They embraced, she thanked him for lunch and then she was out the door as fast as she had come.

DC was aware that Suzanne knew the truth. He wanted to see how King had been affected by his actions and after talking with Suzanne, he felt certain that King would be alright and he could now resume his life.

King was destined to be great, he was also ruthless and dangerous. He already had a body under his belt and had witnessed his first murder. The complicated part about the whole ordeal was that it didn't bother King. That's what scared DC more than anything.

Chapter 3

It had been a month since Chuckie's death and King had been playing with the thought of continuing his uncle's business. Len had sat around the house looking crazy the past couple of weeks. Customers and acquaintances came by and paid their respects as King and Len sat on the porch. They were also looking to score some crack and King contemplated whether he could trust his uncle with something he had found, he had an itch himself that needed to be scratched.

It was a Tuesday and the first of the month was on Thursday. *"Fuck it,"* King thought to himself. He approached Len and told him that he found a package on the way home from the gym. Len looked puzzled at first, not trying to show his excitement. Thinking that the package could be fake, King broke a little piece from the pack instead of giving Len the whole package.

Len took it and scrambled to get inside the house. King sat there, waiting for his uncle for at least 15 to 20 minutes. He was about to go look for Len when he came out the door. Uncle Lens eyes were big as saucers and his mouth was white as powdered doughnuts. King had never seen this side of his uncle, he always thought that Len and Chuckie were hustlers. He came to realize at that moment, that this was his uncles true form was a crackhead!!

Minutes passed and he tried to talk to his uncle but got no response. Len was on cloud nine and his mouth was numb as hell. When he did try to respond, he stuttered repeatedly. King waited patiently for his uncle's high to come down. When he finally did come down a little, Len's first words out his mouth were, "Give me two of those rocks, here comes Marcus."

King snapped out of his thoughts and gave his uncle two nice sized rocks. Len looked at the rocks then back at King. Feeling like they weren't big enough, King asked, "What's the problem?"

Len didn't say a word, he walked away to make the play just as Chuckie would have done. He walked down the block and after making the transaction he came back and sat on the porch.

"Here you go nephew," Len said, giving King $30 and one of the rocks back. Knowing King knew nothing about hustling, Len was about to take him to school. "Let's go in the house so I can school you on how to cut them thangs up," Len stated as he led King into the house.

King handed the pack to his uncle. Len sat at the table and pulled a razor out of his pocket. As he cut the dope into pieces, he held up a rock and explained that it went for $20. Then he showed King another one that went for $10. "Never keep drugs on you and after making a play, never come and sit straight back on the porch. Always get the money first," Uncle Len said with emphasis.

After being in the house for twenty minutes, King felt like he had everything down pat. He also knew he had to apply the 'Laws of the Land' that his father had taught him. He and Len both went back outside and sat on the porch.

As King stayed on the porch keeping his eyes open, Uncle Len spent the day running. By the time Suzanne came home from work, King had accumulated $1,200. He gave his uncle $200 because he didn't want any drugs. Len wanted to show his nephew that he could kick his habit and get back to the money. King wanted his uncle by his side and off drugs.

Eventually Len told King the truth, that he and Chuckie were smokers. It was hard for King to accept at first, he had always seen them get money, not smoke. Len explained that they had always gotten high, just not in his presence.

"I want you to get straight and get this money with me Unc," King stated.

The opportunity to fly straight sounded good to Len. "I'm gonna do right, just don't give up on me," Uncle Len replied.

"Only time will tell," King thought to himself.

Later, King was in his room counting the money, with a million thoughts running through his mind. He had made his first $6,200 at the age of 14. He was ecstatic! What was he going to do with the money? He had plenty of drugs left. King decided that nothing would change, he would continue to go to school and play basketball as normal.

The next couple of weeks went by in a blur. King was in the 8th grade and the school year was coming to an end. His count was now at $10,000 from the package. King had finished the school year, but he had also finished selling the package that he had. He felt that he needed to have a much needed conversation with his father. Uncle Len had stopped smoking crack and AAU would be starting in a couple of weeks. He wanted to get a summer job so that he could spend some money if he wanted to, without being questioned by his mom. Suzanne was proud that her son had passed his grade and would be attending High School the following year.

A week before the summer basketball season was to start, King and his father went on a weekend vacation. DC had taken them down to Myrtle Beach in South Carolina where they jet skied, took helicopter rides, and shopped. On the Sunday they were scheduled to return and were going out to eat before leaving. King decided this was the best time to put everything on the table. DC always told King that they could talk about anything and they both vowed to never lie to one another about anything.

DC sat there quietly and patiently, waiting for his son to let out what he was working up to say. King saw the anxiety on his dad's face, took a deep breath and told his father that he had been selling drugs for the past couple of months. DC wanted to know who had been giving his son drugs to sell, so that he could go kill them. King didn't lie to his father, he told him that he had taken the drugs off his Uncle Chuckie the night he was shot. He also told him about the gun. After seeing how his confession affected his father, he decided to wait a while before he let him know that his other uncle had been helping him.

DC was stunned at the revelation King had just laid on him. He felt he knew everything about everything that was moving in his town. That meant King knew how to move without being seen. He had to admit, he was proud, and a little shocked at the same time. He kept his feelings concealed, he always knew that King would hustle eventually, it was in his blood. He had also seen the way King's eyes lit up when it came to money. His son always talked about saving money and investing it, spending it was never an option. Hell King already had a body under his belt and was out there making money. DC wasn't even selling drugs at all. He was caught between a rock and a hard place with his decision. He sat there, deep in his thoughts for a bit, and then King excused himself to go to the restroom.

When King returned, he noticed his father was still sitting in the same position. He got settled into his seat and waited for his father's reaction.

DC calmly asked him, "What do you want out of life?"

King had been taught to think before he spoke and he took his time replying to his father's question. "I would like to be able to provide for my family and play professional basketball. Then, if for whatever reason that don't work out, I'd like to run a lucrative business, get married and have children. I want to be able to see them grow through life and live happily ever after," King explained.

After hearing King explain what he wanted out of life, DC asked King, "Don't you think that's what I wanted for you?"

King sat there dumb founded. He never looked at it like that. As he thought about it, he realized that his dad was right.

DC exhaled, trying to gather his thoughts. "I want you to go to college, play professional basketball, and I also want you to own a business if basketball doesn't work out. I want you to get married and have me some grandbabies," DC said, his smile lightening the mood. "So my next question is this, where does selling drugs fit into this equation?" He asked, sitting up closer to King.

"I want the money now!" King replied. "I can go to school and play basketball. The money can come on the side as I've been doing for the last couple of months," he said confidently as his father sat back, listening to his son. King continued, "I could get hurt and not be able to play basketball. Dad, all I'm saying is that I know what I wanna do. I know what I've been bred to do. Seeing you get money and have anything you desire, that's driven me to want the same things and more. I've been watching you all my life.

When you talk, I listen. When you move through the crowds and mingle amongst others, I watch every move you make."

DC was surprised to hear the observation that his son had been making. Right then and there he knew the only choice he had was to guide his son to the top. Legally and illegally. There wasn't no use in denying him what he wanted, his young mind was already made up and denying him would fuel his flame and make him do it anyway.

"Well I've made my decision," DC said.

King prayed his dad was sold on his speech. He sat up, anxiously awaiting his father's reply. "I'm listening," King said, sounding defeated.

"Let's get it!" DC said looking King in the eyes with a serious scowl on his face.

Chapter 4

It was summer, 1996 and school was out for break. Everybody in the city was out trying to be seen. King had a birthday coming up the next month. His most recent basketball game left him scoring a season high of 21 points. He also had the best work in the hood. When school started back in the fall, he would be a freshman in High School.

After DC's blessing, King started hustling hard. Standing at 6'1" and weighing 185 pounds, with cornrows and the body of a God, King had it going on. He invested $9,000 into himself to keep appearances and get business started. DC gave him 18 ounces, 9 of them were on consignment. Uncle Len cooked the work for him in a spot he had opened up on the Eastside. King's decision to take things there was to keep traffic away from his house and his mom.

King had a homeboy on the Eastside named Twan. He and Twan had grown up together but Twan had moved from the Westside. They were inseparable. Twan had a little spot he was running on E. Fisher Street. He, King, and Uncle Len would spend their time sitting outside on the porch. Uncle Len would do most of the running. Even though he wasn't smoking anymore, he still knew most of the smokers. Things were going real smooth.

They only sold 20's and up. If a smoker had $50 they would get four rocks. $75 to $80 would get them a whole gram. Some days there would be so many smokers out there that King and Twan could get lost in the crowd. Other hustlers on the block couldn't compete with the product, or the prices King had and King knew that the other hustlers were missing money because of him. The reality of the conversations he and his father had were coming to fruition.

King didn't want to make enemies by taking money out of their pockets, or make them feel as though he was stepping on their toes. So he decided to bring them in on his team. He started selling them ounces for $900. He was taking a $300 loss but he made up for it on the backend. He would take an ounce and cook it up, stretching it to 44 grams. That's how raw the cocaine was. He could sell the ounce and still have 16 grams extra.

After hitting off the other hustlers on the block, King and Twan would branch out to another block on the Eastside. They would sell 20's and up, then muscle the block with their product. They would then give hustlers on the block the $900. Going from block to block on the Eastside with that scheme, the trio made it work.

Every hustler that was on the block before they came ended up getting down with their crew. Twan had started selling weed and King and Uncle Len remained selling work. King had built a nice team of hustlers who would come to be known as NAAM, 'Niggas All About Money'. There were five of them in all and they were all young, money making, respected hustlers.

No matter what happened, or where they went, Uncle Len was rolling with the youngins. On days that King had basketball practice, or a game, Uncle Len would take control of the operation. The money was flowing and everybody was happy. As everyone knows, the more money you get, the more problems come with it.

King and his team had avoided numerous problems. Two weeks before King's 15th birthday, they were at a barber shop on the Eastside, by the Brookview apartments. It was a known hotspot. Twan and King had been getting their haircut for the weekend and King was actually standing outside waiting on Twan to get finished when he saw a group of guys that gang banged the area. The leader of the group, known as "Five", felt King was trying to take over their turf.

He approached King aggressively. "What's popping?" Five asked.

"Ain't shit," King replied. "Waiting on my partna' to finish getting his haircut."

"Oh. Ok. I was just checking, I know how you be moving," Five said, looking at King with a mean mug.

"Wow, it ain't even like that homie," King stated. King always felt the animosity whenever he and Twan came to get their haircuts on Fridays. He knew he had to kill the problem before it became one. "What y'all be moving over here anyway?" King asked.

"Just a lil work," Five stated.

Five had his lil homie, Smoke, with him. Smoke never liked King because of a lil chick named Candy. Smoke was feeling Candy until she told him that 'he ain't getting money like King'. There wasn't shit he could do for her. King had been smashing the pussy for a while now.

"How about you give me a call to see IF we can work something out?" King tested.

"That's respect," Five answered.

"What's good?" Twan said, stepping out of the barbershop and feeling tension in the air.

"What you mean what's good?" Smoke questioned, visibly clutching the pistol on his waist.

"Calm yo ass down," Five said, checking his lil shooter.

Twan was a livewire himself. Standing 5'10", with light skin and a pretty boy face, he was 150 pounds soaking wet. You wouldn't have thought he was much if you didn't know the demons he had in his closet.

"You always fucking some shit up," Five said, chastising him.

As the young men went their separate ways, King said to Twan, "We're gonna have to kill Five and Smoke."

Twan replied, "Let's get it!"

King knew Smoke's weakness was Candy. He would use her to set Smoke up, then he and Twan would be able to get Five by himself and take care of him.

Later that night Candy called Smoke to her crib. She stayed in an apartment on the Westside called The Civics. Everybody knew about Civics. Every hood rat in Salisbury had stayed at the Civics, from the top to the bottom.

King had told Candy to act like she was gonna give Smoke some pussy, then he waited for the perfect moment. King was sitting outside as Smoke walked nervously up to Candy's door. He looked around suspiciously as he clutched his gun. After knocking on the door repeatedly, Candy appeared. She opened the door in just a T-shirt and panties and Smoke almost knocked her down trying to get into the house. He was scared to be seen going into her apartment, but excited about getting some pussy at the same time.

Now that Smoke was tied down, King could handle his other business. He dialed Five's number and Five answered immediately. "What's popping?" He responded.

"Trying to catch up with you so we can chop it up about that twerk," King said.

"Dats cool, meet me at the barbershop," Five instructed.

"Okay. But what it do?" King asked, checking for his order.

"One-time," Five replied, stating that he would take one brick.

King smiled to himself as he thought, *"Damn, I'ma get some money off this nigga after I smoke his ass."* Then he said, "Okay! That's gonna be $29 and I'ma shoot you one to go with it." King had lied, *"You always gotta give them an offer they can't refuse,"* King thought to himself.

"You ain't gotta do all that King. If it's good I'ma rock with you. I'm on my way," Five told him as he hung up.

King called Twan and gave him the run down. Ten minutes later King pulled up to the barbershop in a car he had rented from a crackhead for the occasion. King got out of the car and sat on the hood. After texting Candy to see what was going on there, Twan suddenly appeared out of nowhere.

"What's good," Five said, approaching King.

King stood up off the hood and put his hands inside his hoodie.

"Where ya partna at?" Five asked.

"Probably in some pussy somewhere," King lied.

"You and that nigga don't go nowhere without each other," Five started getting a funny feeling.

"Aye! This is some drop," King said, changing the subject and handing a brick to him.

Five took the work from King and looked it over, then put it up to his nose. After smelling the pure cocaine through the wrapper, Five reached into his hoodie and pulled out a brown paper bag. "That's $29,000 and not a dollar short," Five stated, tossing the bag to King.

"I have the other brick as well, if you want it," King said.

Five accepted it since King had brought it and told him that he could pick his money up tomorrow. They gave each other a pound, then King turned and got back into the car.

As he started to pull away from the barber shop, Five was just getting to the corner of the building. Out of nowhere gun shots rang out in the dark. Looking in his rearview mirror, King could see Five drop to the ground and Twan run up to go through his pockets.

As King pulled away Candy text and said she was high as hell so she was about to put Smoke's ass out. King text back and said ok, that he would see her tomorrow. King was headed back to the Westside when Twan called. He answered and told Twan to meet him at the crib.

When he pulled up to the crib Twan was sitting on the porch smoking a blunt. He got out of the car and started laughing as he saw how nonchalant Twan was acting, as if nothing had taken place. They knew nothing of the bodies each of them had already caught. King thought this was Twan's first.

"Let me hit that shit," King said, reaching for the blunt. "Did you do what I asked?" King questioned.

"Yes, I did," Twan said, handing back the brick." I dropped some of the coke at the crime scene and a blue do-rag."

"Okay! That's what's up." King handed Twan back the brick and told him he could have it.

They smoked the blunt and then King told Twan to go burn the rental. They gave each other a pound and went their separate ways, both satisfied with a day's work.

Chapter 5

June 24th, 1996 was Kings 15th birthday. Suzanne woke King up at 8:00 am and to his surprise, DC was downstairs at the kitchen table, along with Twan, Uncle Len, and Candy. They all sat around the kitchen table with enough food to feed a small army. This had been a ritual since he was 13, with the exception of Candy and Uncle Chuckie not being there. Candy had become a permanent fixture in King's life.

The murder of Five had not been linked to Twan or King. Word on the streets and the police were reporting that it was gang related, considering there was a blue do-rag at the crime scene. It could have also just been a robbery gone wrong with the amount of cocaine that was found at the scene.

King ate breakfast with his loved ones as the conversation turned to plans that had been made for the day. They would have a surprise for King later that night, but he didn't know it yet. They finished breakfast and DC told everyone to come outside. They all got up and made their way to the front door as a car pulled up in front of the house.

King opened the door to see a black Cadillac DeVille with a red bowtie on the top of it sitting at the curb. DC's right hand, Kareem, got out of the car with a Kool-Aid smile and walked up to the porch. He stood beside DC, and then handed the keys to King with the same smile. King took the keys and gave Kareem a hug. He turned to his father with a grateful look and hugged him.

"Happy Birthday son. This is a gift from your mother and I both. We hope you enjoy it!"

Suzanne didn't want DC to pay for the car alone, even though he could have. This was Kings first car and she wanted him to say that he got his first car from both his parents. DC understood the significance in her approach.

King jumped in the car, followed by Twan in the back and Candy riding in the passenger seat. They rode around Salisbury and down Long Street with the music blasting. Twan got dropped off at one of their spots on the Eastside, then Candy and King went and got a room at the Chanticleer Motel in Spencer. It was still early but King wanted some pussy before he got his day started, they hadn't been together sexually in almost two weeks.

Once they got into the room, Candy sat on the bed and rolled a blunt. King laid across the bed and started receiving multiple pages on his beeper. There were so many pages that he decided they would smoke the blunt and leave. Candy was past upset to say the least, she had looked forward to smoking the blunt and having birthday sex. She already knew that once they left the room there was no guarantee that she would see him again until that night.

After they finished smoking the blunt and talked about events for the day, King drove her home. He kissed her goodbye and agreed they would see other later, then Candy got out of the car and went into her apartment.

King drove to his house to take a shower and get ready to start his day. When he pulled up Uncle Len and his mom were in a heated discussion. Apparently a couple of crackheads had come to the house to buy some crack. Uncle Len had been trying to defend King.

Suzanne approached King, distraught, but King put her accusations to rest by denying her suspicions. Uncle Len said that they saw him sitting on the porch and assumed that the block was back to pumping. Seeing King around the house gave them the perception that one of them had drugs. The issue was resolved for the day, but later on down the road, it would arise again.

Later that day King and Uncle Len were cruising around on the Eastside. King rode with Uncle Len, considering he didn't have a license. They pulled up to the spot on E. Shave Street and sat on the porch with Twan. Everybody was coming through to see what King had planned for that night, he was the Prince of the East and the son of a kingpin. Everyone expected a big birthday bash.

DC had told King to meet up with him at Christo's. An Italian restaurant that was known for their famous chicken wings.

"Let's hit the mall before it gets late," Twan suggested.

"Let's ride," King stated as the men got up and got in the car.

Time seemed to be moving really fast. Time fly's when you're having fun.

By the time they left the mall, it was already 6:30 pm. They had to be at Christo's at 7:00 pm and they were running out of time.

"Let's just go to my house," Twan demanded. "That way we don't have to ride all the way to the Westside and back."

Twan stayed on the Eastside in some apartment called the Lincoln. It was 7:15 by the time both the men had gotten dressed. After making sure that he was dressed immaculately, King looked into the mirror. He had on some all-white, Air Force One's and a white, Polo linen short set. He also donned a Cuban link necklace with the matching bracelet. The boy looked like money. Never to be outdone!

Twan was just as fly as King. Everything about him was the total opposite, it's just how they were, night and day. Twan rocked the all-black Air Force One's, with the all-black linen short set. He wasn't into jewelry, but, he sported a Figaro chain with an iced out Jesus charm piece.

King's pager had gone off ten minutes later, Uncle Len was outside to pick them up and carry them to Christo's. The closer they got, the more hyper they became. Twan was in the backseat, rolling a phat blunt and they smoked as they rode.

When they got there it was jammed packed. Len drove around the parking lot several times, but there wasn't anywhere for them to park and King recognized several cars there. King looked at Uncle Len and said, "You knew about this didn't you?"

Len just smiled and shook his head.

Suzanne stood outside the entrance waiting for them, she was decked out in an all-white Christian Dior dress with white Dior heels. DC was with her and he was draped in an all-white Armani suit. Seeing his mother and father together like this made King happy, even if it was only for the night, they looked really good together.

Beside his mother stood Candy in a black, green, and red, Gucci dress that was so tight you could see her heart beat. She had on the matching flip-flops and she was stunning.

King got out of the car, followed by Twan and Uncle Len. Everyone immediately started singing happy birthday as he walked in. They had somehow all piled into the restaurant, along with the others.

There was pizza, wings, Alfredo, and salad being served but King couldn't get comfortable, he was constantly interrupted by everyone wanting to come show him love for his born day. He was handed numerous cards with money, along with gifts that were wrapped and even bands of cash.

Seeing all this made Suzanne reflect on the altercation with Len earlier. There were faces there that she didn't know, or recognize, even though she knew their parents through mutual friends. A lot of them were hustlers and she knew it. She knew she was gonna have to talk to her son, but now wasn't the time, or the place. Not with everything that was going on.

Nobody saw Smoke, tucked off in the corner, watching King and Candy. Smoke thought Candy was really feeling him. The night he went to her crib she didn't let him fuck her. She only let him play with the pussy and eat it until she got her nut. He felt played and he didn't like it. He vowed to destroy King and get back at her. Whether it would be to kill King or something else, he would destroy him. He was determined for them to feel his wrath. Smoke also had a feeling that King was responsible for killing Five, but he couldn't prove it.

They all partied until 10pm, then everyone went their separate ways. That night was King's introduction into the game. His life would forever change after the summer of 1996.

Chapter 6

When school started back that fall, King was excited, he had spent most of the summer perfecting his game. His AAU team made it to the championship and lost to Florida. AAU was a summer league that helped players prepare for the upcoming school season. He was more than ready.

He had also gotten his driver's permit, which allowed him to drive after hours as long as somebody in the car had a license. Candy was constantly by his side and by that time, Twan had permanently dropped out of school. King tried to coax his partner to come and get his education, but Twan had gotten attached to the streets. King didn't plan on selling drugs forever, he had a seven year plan that would get him in and out, unscathed! For whatever reason, if it didn't pan out, he could fall back on his education. At the moment, things were on track to go according to his planed. Money was good and King and his mom had moved. His team had started seeing money and Uncle Len had gotten completely off drugs.

It was the end of the first day of school and King had just headed for home. As he looked down his phone rang. It was DC so King instantly felt that something was wrong. DC wanted to meet at a restaurant nearby so King picked up Twan and drove straight there. He pulled up to Ham's Restaurant on E. Innes Street and they got out. He didn't know if it was a good idea to bring Twan, but DC knew they were inseparable. He actually looked at Twan as another son.

The young men waltzed into the restaurant to find DC sitting in a back booth with Kareem. DC stood up and they greeted each other. After pleasantries were exchanged, DC got straight to it.

"Somebody shot at me last night while I was walking into my house," he stated.

King sat there and listened as his blood boiled. *"Who would be stupid enough to try that and not succeed?"* King thought to himself. "Do y'all have any idea who it was?" King asked.

"Yes! It's Shane's brother. He was released two days ago. He has it in his mind that I killed Shane."

Neither King nor his father had spoken of that night since it happened. So hearing Shane's name now, brought back memories.

"Ok, well what's the move, since we know who it is?" King asked.

"The streets are buzzing. Everyone's waiting for my reaction," DC explained. "The boy is trying to make a name for himself and he wants to use me to do it," DC said, hitting the table with a balled-up fist. "I've dealt with his kind before and it wasn't pretty," DC reminisced. "He isn't the first person to come for my crown and I'm sure he won't be the last. I'm bringing this to your attention so that you will be aware." DC slid a piece of paper across the table.

King took the paper and noticed it was a picture.

"That is who shot at me," DC said, answering King's question before he could ask it.

King slid the paper to Twan so he could lock the face into his memory bank.

"I'm gonna leave town for a couple of days to let things cool down. In the meantime, I want you off the blocks. Focus on school and basketball. This problem should be taken care of by the time I return," DC said while looking at Kareem.

King understood the subliminal message that had just been sent and he was already formulating his own plan. He played it cool. "Okay Dad, I'll lay low and maintain. The block has been hot lately anyway," he lied. "Them lil Westside niggas been on some BS anyway," King added.

"Well, I'll be in touch. I'm about to head to Charlotte, my plane leaves in two hours. I'm going to West Virginia to visit some old friends," DC said.

Everybody stood and gave parting hugs and pounds.

"Be safe, I love you Dad," King told his father.

"Always son! You and Twan be safe as well," DC told them.

"Yes Sir Mr. Cummings," Twan replied.

"Later," said Kareem as the boys walked out of the restaurant.

Soon as they got inside the car Twan said, "You already know."

"Let's get it," King replied with a mean mug on his face.

It was nightfall and King had paged his lil homies, Skinny, Grinch, and Revlon. They made up the NAAM crew. Nobody took them serious, but these five young killers couldn't be played with, or taken for granted. Every last one of them had done put down a mean demonstration to earn respect.

King and Twan sat at the House of Prayer basketball court, waiting on the others to pull up. King was still baffled that someone had shot at his father. Skinny was the first to pull up, followed by Grinch ten minutes later. Revlon was the last to show up as usual, he was the busy one out of the crew.

Twan was shooting baskets as the men walked onto the court. They passed blunts and caught up with what the others had going on. When the blunts were gone, King got down to business.

"Look I'm glad that everyone was able to make it. This nigga that just came home two days ago shot at my father last night," King explained. Everyone knew there was more, so no one spoke. "The guy that did it thinks my pops killed his brother." King reached inside his pocket and pulled out the picture. He passed it around so everyone could lock it in. "He calls himself Slug, and I think he's a problem that needs to be dealt with," King confessed.

"Aye! I know dude!" Skinny said. "He be with them Westside niggas. They came riding through the East earlier. They wasn't on shit," Skinny said nonchalantly.

"We need all the info we can get on dude, but my dad told me to fall back," said King.

"Ain't no way!" Revlon exclaimed. "We gonna handle this!"

King was the only one that went to school out of all the goons. They were all eating because of him, so they felt it was their duty to handle anything and everything that came his way.

"King you're the bait," Twan explained. "Tomorrow I want you to post up on the block. Once Slug see you, he got one chance to get at you," Twan continued. "So be on your A game! After he makes his move on you, and you don't kill him on sight. We will follow him and see where he leads us. Hopefully it's somewhere that he lays his head. Then we will kill him before your father returns," Twan finished explaining his plan.

Grinch was maybe two years older than everybody else. He was also the thinker out of the group. "So how do you feel about that?" He questioned King.

"It sounds good," King answered.

"I'll be there with you," Twan stated, letting King know that he would put himself in the line of fire as well.

"I appreciate that," King said, dapping Twan up. "When we catch him, we're not gonna kill him," King ordered. "I have bigger plans for him."

They rolled up a few blunts and continued to talk. They hadn't really seen each other in days. King had been in school, while everyone else had been doing their own thing.

King's pager went off and after looking at the number, he yelled, "Yo! I'll catch y'all tomorrow!"

Everyone said their goodbyes and then Twan and King jumped in the Lac and peeled out.

"What's good?" Twan asked as King drove recklessly through traffic.

King didn't answered he just drove quietly the whole way to his house. He and his mom had moved to the outskirts of Salisbury, to West Cliff. When they pulled up, King jumped out of the car and ran into the house with Twan right on his heels.

When they got into the house King saw Uncle Len laying on the couch with blood all over him. "What's good Unc?" King asked, breathing rapidly.

"Me and that young boy Slug, got into a fight," Len replied.

King couldn't believe his ears.

"So where did all the blood come from?" Twan asked.

"The nigga stabbed me in my shoulder," Uncle Len cried out in pain.

"Where's my mom?" King asked, looking around the house frantically.

"I'm right here," Suzanne retorted, coming up the hallway with the first aid kit. "Call your father," she stated, looking directly at King.

"No!" Uncle Len shouted. "I'm ok. Leave DC outta this. I can handle it," Len insisted.

"You are the only brother DC has left. I don't wanna see you hurt or worse, and I don't wanna see you hurt anybody else," Suzanne said sincerely.

"Thank you for your concern, but I can handle this," Len said humbly.

"Come on Unc, let's go to the basement. I'll help you get cleaned up," King said as he helped Len up from the couch.

Twan went upstairs to Kings room, to grab Uncle Len a shirt, then the trio met in the basement where King started cleaning his uncle's wound. Len finished telling them how the altercation started and they all listened.

By the time King had finished cleaning the wound, Twan had devised a deadly plan. King didn't like the plan because it didn't include him. He told Len about his dad getting shot at the night before and Len was devastated.

Len didn't mention that Slug had made it clear that he would kill anybody who was associated with DC. He wanted King to be able to continue to go to school. Len and Twan would get with the rest of the crew and strategize a plan to get rid of Slug tomorrow. It couldn't wait, the nigga had to go. He had crossed the two most important and influential people in Kings life.

Twan and Uncle Len sat with King and smoked a few blunts, then they both excused themselves. King had some homework that needed to be done anyway, so he went to his room.

Before going to bed that night, King called his father. They talked for about 30 minutes while DC informed him about what had happened to Uncle Len. King played dumb as if he wasn't already aware of the situation. They promised to talk as soon as King got out of school the next day and then ended the conversation. King laid in bed for a long time, thinking about what tomorrow would bring.

Chapter 7

For the last week King had been going to school and basketball practice daily. He hadn't been to the block since Twan and Uncle Len left his house together. There hadn't been any sightings of Slug anywhere. He had just been chilling like his father asked him to.

Twan and the crew had been on the block, going hard, hoping Slug would come through so they could crush him. It had been over a week and no one knew where he laid his head or had seen him anywhere.

King was on his way out of practice and headed to pick up Candy when he noticed Slug parked right beside his car, smoking a blunt with other guys. King found himself face to face with the guy responsible for shooting at his father and stabbing his uncle. His first thought was to swing on the nigga, but patience is a virtue, so he would let Slug make the first move.

Without hesitation, King walked straight up to his car like slug wasn't even there. He put his key into the door and heard Slug break the silence.

"What's up youngin?" Slug asked.

"Ain't shit. What's good?" King replied while unlocking his car door.

"Just came to have a word with you," Slug stated.

"No disrespect, but do I know you?" King questioned, playing it real smooth.

Slug wasn't expecting things to go like this. Evidently King didn't know who Slug was. Or so he thought! "No! We don't know each other and that is why I'm here. My name is Slug and I'm Shane's youngest brother. From my understanding, it was your father that killed my brother," Slug confessed.

Hearing this made all King's senses stand on high alert. Slug stood almost 6'6" and King was a little over 6' himself. They stood eye to eye, even though they were several feet apart.

Slug was just about to speak when King cut him off. "For you to be standing here making detrimental accusations like this, you must have some kind of proof," King inquired.

Slug didn't have any proof. He had only been home two weeks so he was going off word on the streets. Sensing the hostility in King's voice put Slug on the defensive. As he thought about what King said, the aggressiveness seemed to fade from him. Slug already had it in his mind that DC was the killer. He shot at DC and tried to kill him, then stabbed his brother. The lines of disrespect had already been crossed.

"To answer your question, no. I don't have any solid proof, just word of mouth. I'm here because I want you to reach out to your pops and tell him we have to have a sit down," explained Slug.

King could not believe what he was hearing. *This nigga must really think that I'm green,* King thought to himself. He started laughing hysterically and the laughter caught Slug off guard.

"What's funny?" Slug asked, sounding offended.

"For you to think that my father would have a sit down with you," was what he was thinking. Instead King said, "You thinking my father killed your brother. No disrespect towards your brother,

but my father has too much to lose to be out there killing somebody that can't make his status or fortune rise. But considering you asked, I'll see what he says," King stated. "It's somewhere I gotta be, so I'll catch you later."

"Alright! You do that," Slug replied, obviously upset.

King got into his car and pulled off. The other guys with Slug sat on the car shaking their heads.

"What is it?" Slug asked.

The nigga with the dreads spoke up, his name was Juice. "Man! You know you should have killed that boy. That lil nigga run the whole Eastside."

"And!?" Slug yelled. "He ain't no fucking threat. That lil nigga thinking about playing basketball and fucking some whores. I got this nigga!" Slug spouted, beating his chest.

"If you say so big brah," Juice said.

Sitting in the darkest shadows and unseen by anyone, Twan and Skinny were parked three rows down from Slug. They had been there every day after King got out of school. They knew Slug would show up sometime, now all they had to do was follow him.

Slug and his goons got in their car and pulled out of the school's parking lot. Twan followed behind them slowly, letting two cars separate them. They traveled down W. Caldwell Street as Skinny got on his cell phone. They followed Slug and his goons all the way out by the mall and eventually turned into some apartments called Clancy Hills.

Slug slowly turned into the middle section and Twan kept going straight. Twan made a right turn into the last section and after making sure nobody was on to them, Twan found a spot and parked. Skinny hung the phone up and told Twan that Uncle Len was on his way. From where they were parked he could see straight into the middle section, but they had no idea which apartment the trio had went into.

Twenty minutes later, Uncle Len pulled up with a look on his face that neither of them had ever seen. Uncle Len was out for blood. They didn't know it was him at first, he was in a crackheads car and it didn't have a tag on it. He rolled the window down and signaled for them to get in with him. Once they were in Uncle Len rode up and down the strip five or six times hashing the whole thing out. The plan had to be fool proof.

Feeling that things were explained well enough, they let Twan out at his car. Skinny and Uncle Len rode down to the middle section and as soon as Slug came outside to get in his car they were gonna smash him.

They sat in their cars for two, almost three hours and it was starting to get to them. They had to get their man. It was almost 7pm and starting to get dark outside when Skinny started dosing off. He was woken by Uncle Len telling him to get ready. Skinny quickly sat up in his seat and saw the man standing in the hallway talking. All of Skinny's senses were suddenly wide awake.

Both men cocked their pistols and got out of the car. Uncle Len had on a black hoodie, and Skinny had on a black champion jacket and a fitted hat. As they watched the men continue conversing, Twan passed down the breezeway from the last section. The trio were headed to the black Altima that they arrived in.

Len waited until all three man had gotten into the car and got comfortable. Then Twan, Len, and Skinny surrounded the car before they could turn the ignition. Seeing all three of them sent Slug into panic mode, but before he could even beg for his life, they

Swiss cheesed the car. There were at least ten rounds let off into the car, guaranteeing closed caskets.

Once outta bullets, all three men ran back to Twan's car. As they were running off, some chick came out of one of the apartments. Twan turned and shot at her, sending her back inside. She didn't see the car that they had gotten back into and the crackhead car was left behind. Len, Skinny, and Twan jumped in the car and were out. They made a clean get away!

Chapter 8

DC had just landed at Charlotte International Airport where Kareem was in the terminal waiting for his friend to walk off the plane. Kareem had just found out that Slug and two of his home boys had been gunned down a couple of days ago. He informed DC, who was happy to hear the news. He got straight on another plane, headed back to Salisbury.

Slug getting killed wasn't the reason for cutting his vacation short. The vacation was cut short because Kareem wasn't the one who had killed him. Hell! Kareem hadn't seen Slug the whole time DC had been gone. DC looked at the situation as an embarrassment. The streets would look at DC as if he were getting soft, like he wasn't the King of the jungle anymore.

As DC departed from the plane in Salisbury and entered the terminal, his anger could be felt in each stride he took, they were long, powerful, and purposeful. Kareem didn't know what to expect from his longtime friend. There was never a task that he wasn't able to complete, but this one seemed impossible.

"How was the flight?" Kareem asked, taking DC's luggage.

"Frustrating," DC answered with one short word.

As they rushed out of the terminal, people stared at Kareem as he tried to keep up with DC, it was a sight to see. Kareem looked as if he were damn near chasing him.

Once they got outside and finally reached the car, DC exploded! "Now tell me what the fuck is going on?" He demanded.

They got in and Kareem put the car into drive. As he drove, he replayed the conversation that the chick had with him to DC.

"So this nigga had other beefs going on besides with me?" DC snapped.

"Apparently because she said that three niggas ran down on them and shot the car about 100 times," Kareem stated, looking at his friend in the rearview mirror. Kareem was distraught that he had let DC down and it showed on his face. He had bags under his eyes, indicating he hadn't gotten any sleep.

Rubbing his head in frustration, DC was happy but also confused. He didn't know who to thank or give credit to. Being the HNIC and not being able to handle certain situations, only made you food on a plate. DC didn't have any flaws and would hate for anyone to find one in his armor. That would only put him at risk of jeopardizing all he had worked so hard to accumulate.

"I understand what you may be feeling," Kareem said, interrupting DC's thoughts.

"I'll get to the bottom of this," DC assured. "That's a promise!"

DC knew that Kareem was loyal, honest, and more than capable of handling any situation. He just didn't like not knowing what was going on around him. As they rode, DC instructed him to go to King's house. Uncle Len and the crew were on the Eastside. They had gotten back to hustling and King was right beside them.

"So what happened to Slug?" King questioned.

King had been in the blind since the conversation he had with Slug at the school that day. Neither Twan nor Uncle Len had spoken a word about it, but when King asked they would inform him on the details.

"We knew Slug wasn't gonna show back up on the Eastside. He and Uncle Len had just gotten into it. The only other person for him to get at was you," Twan said, pointing his finger at King. "So me and Skinny decided to watch your back while you were in school and when you went to basketball practice."

King looked puzzled as he scrunched up his face. He was always aware of his surroundings but not once had he spotted Skinny or Twan while he was in school.

"We watched your car and the parking lot every day," Twan continued. "While you were in practice we would sit on your car and flirt with the cheerleaders." Twan laughed as he told the story, but he knew that it was making King very uncomfortable. King felt like he was slipping. "Then the other day our patience finally paid off, Slug showed up in the lot. We were optimistic about how you would kill him and his homeboys in the parking lot, but we knew that there are cameras outside the gym. So we just sat and let y'all converse."

"I ain't gonna lie," King chimed in. "I thought he was gonna try and shoot me! He already had the drop on me," King said as he dropped his head, replaying the situation.

"I was scared too," Skinny said, standing up.

"You played it like a G though," Twan said with a smirk on his face. "My admiration for you sky rocketed after witnessing that," Twan admitted. "If that nigga would have shot you, I don't know what I would have done," Twan said shaking his head.

King laughed it off after replying, "Ya boy was scared as hell!" Everyone erupted in laughter. "So finish the story nigga," King said wanting the details.

"We followed him from the school, all the way to Clancy Hills. Then we called Uncle Len," Twan said.

King looked at Uncle Len, who shrugged his shoulders as if to say, 'I did what I had to do'.

"Brah we sat out at that bitch for five hours," Twan complained, hitting his palm in frustration at the time they had put in.

The sun had gone down and Skinny's high ass was going to sleep.

Uncle Len interrupted, "Hell yeah! I smoked a whole box of Philly's waiting on his bitch ass to come outside."

"When they came out I saw that it was Slug and the same two niggas that was with him at the school. I couldn't see Skinny and Uncle," Twan explained. "But I knew they were manning just as I was. I got out of my car and started moving towards them. As I'm approaching, I see Skinny and Uncle Len creeping. The men started piling into a black Altima," Twan continued.

"They were sitting ducks," Uncle Len said, adding his two cents.

"The only reason we got the drop on them was because it had gotten dark," Skinny added.

"Once they got comfortable we surrounded that bitch and all hell broke loose," Twan said as he pounded Uncle Len and Twan.

"Skinny started acting as if he was at a shooting gallery. He started swinging an imaginary chopper back and forth.

"I know every bullet that we shot hit one of them niggas," Uncle Len stated.

"Damn," Uncle Len said, jumping as if he'd gotten shocked. "I gotta go get that damn crackhead car."

"Hell naw! Let the smoker go get it himself!" King yelled. "Somebody might remember you from the shooting and call the police."

"Yeah! You right," Uncle Len replied.

"How did you forget about the car?" Twan asked.

"For real, fuck that car," Uncle Len replied sarcastically.

"Yo! Ain't that Quick?" Skinny asked.

Everybody looked up to see Quick pulling up in a 325 Benz. He parked and got out of the car looking like money. When he approached he spoke to everyone.

"Aye! Can I holla at you for a minute King?" He asked.

King got up and motioned for Quick to follow him into the house. When they got to the kitchen King said, "How may I help you OG?"

Reaching into his pockets, Quick pulled out a large amount of cash. He counted out $1,800 and passed it to King. "That's the money for the two zones that you gave me. I would like to grab some more if it's possible," Quick stated.

King counted the money then told him to wait. King walked out of kitchen and came back within minutes. He handed Quick a package and told him that it was four and a baby, meaning four and a half ounces. "You owe me $3,600 and I threw you an extra halftime for being a man of your word," King stated.

Quick started smiling instantly. "Ok that's cool, I'll see you in a couple days," Quick said as he turned to leave. "Oh! Before I leave, let me tell you good luck against North Rowan next week," Quick added, giving King a pound. "I know this is gonna be your first high school game."

"Thanks," King said as the men went back outside.

"Alright, y'all fellas be safe out there," Quick said as he strolled back to his car.

"Peace!" Everyone called out in unison.

Quick had been gone maybe five minutes before DC and Kareem pulled up. Everybody looked toward Uncle Len.

"I'll handle this," Len said, standing up. "Don't nobody mention anything to do with Slug," Uncle Len demanded.

DC and Kareem got out of the car and everyone became nervous.

"Yo! We got our first game coming up next week against North," King said, starting a light conversation.

"I'ma make a run," Kareem said to DC, then he turned around and got back in the car and pulled off. Kareem wanted to stay and see how the conversation went, but DC wanted him to take his luggage to the crib and go to the liquor store to grab a bottle of Crown Royal Black.

"What's up pops?" King questioned.

Everybody said their 'what's ups!' and DC responded, "Chilling! Glad to be back. What's good around here?" He asked, getting straight to the point.

"Let's go into the house," Len spoke up. "Your block day is over," he said with a light chuckle, trying to ease some of the tension that was in the air.

"King, come inside with us," DC instructed.

"No, let him stay outside," Len cut in. "I think you and I need to go talk," Len retorted.

"It's cool dad. Go ahead and talk with Unc," King replied dismissively.

"*This isn't looking good,*" DC thought to himself. "*Why didn't King wanna be a part of this conversation?*"

The men entered the house even thought it was a trap spot. The house was immaculate to say the least. A 55 inch, flat screen was on the wall and the carpet was a six inch plush that you thought might be clouds when you walked on it. Tiffany lamps sat on Ivory end tables and the furniture was top of the line from Ashley's.

As DC sat down, Len asked if he wanted something to drink.

"Sure if it's Crown Royal," DC answered.

It wasn't, so Len took a shot to the head of Jose' Cuervo Gold for himself. After taking his shot Len asked, "What is it that you wanted to talk about?"

DC really wanted King in there so that he could lead the conversation. "I wanna know about the demise of the problem I had," DC stated.

"I'm not gonna lie to you. I never have and I never will," Len said, looking his brother straight in the eyes. "Me and two of the young bulls took care of it," Len confessed nonchalantly. "King didn't have anything to do with it," he added, assuring DC that his son was never put in any danger.

"How is it that y'all could find him, but Kareem couldn't?" DC asked the million dollar question.

"Honestly we didn't have to find him, he came to us. Well, he visited King at school after his altercation with me," Len admitted. "Twan and Skinny were shadowing King when Slug approached him, wanting to have a conversation. We followed him to Clancy Hills and when the opportunity presented itself, we took it," Len explained calmly.

"And nobody seen y'all or knew it was y'all that did it?" DC asked, not believing this.

"No! Not to my knowledge."

"Twan! Y'all get in here!" DC yelled with authority.

The young men filed into the house, one after another. Once everybody was inside and sitting down, DC looked at the young men with admiration.

"May I speak?" Twan asked.

"Of course you can," DC said.

"Mr. Carter, I want to say that we all know you're capable of handling your own situations, first and foremost. You and King are the only family that we have and I speak for both of us when I say this," Twan said humbly. "Even Revlon, though he isn't here right now. Y'all take care of us. Yes we hustle for everything that we obtain, but we're able to hustle because of y'all. When that nigga shot at you and stabbed Uncle Len, it was a no brainer that he had to go. If roles were reversed, I'm sure you would do the same for us. With all respect Mr. Carter, take what we've done as a token of our loyalty to you and King."

DC was stunned by the charisma and morals that these young thugs had inherited. "Thank you Twan, Skinny and you too, my brother," DC said as he put his hand on Len's shoulder. "I love all of you guys, we are family. Blood doesn't make us family, loyalty does," DC said. "For what you have done, I must say thank you." DC looked at them and for the first time he noticed that they were men. "This incident isn't to ever be talked about, or bragged about. It never happened," DC said sternly as he looked at each of them. "Also, I want y'all to get rid of them guns and I'll get some new ones to replace them."

King sat and watched as DC took command of his soldiers.

After DC finished with the serious part of his speech, he ended by saying, "Y'all some gangsta ass lil niggas. These older guys better be careful. I can see y'all taking over in the years to come." DC cracked up laughing and everyone else followed suit, laughing and cutting up. He knew that King would be taking over soon and he was okay with it. There would always be sacrifices for a hustler to make.

Chapter 9

Kings team ended up winning their first game against their rivals, North Rowan. King scored 19 unanswered points for his team that night. He also had 3 steals and 10 assists, he had an awesome debut.

The murder of Slug had happened two weeks earlier and since school had started, King had fallen back from the block. Twan and the crew had been holding things down while King had been spending some quality time with Candy and focusing on his future. Candy had been fucking, and sucking the soul out of him. She wanted to have sex non-stop, daily. They also had a daily ritual of eating at KFC, that girl loved her some chicken tenders and mashed potatoes.

Out of nowhere Suzanne had started to slowly become ill. King first noticed it one day when he and Candy had skipped school. He came out of his room like he was the King of the jungle, butt naked, dick swinging and balls hanging. Suzanne had just come from the doctor's office and was sitting at the kitchen table, reading some pamphlets on cancer.

King walked right into the kitchen, unaware that his mom was home. Suzanne looked up to see the boy walking in butter ball naked. "King!" She shouted.

Stunned, King stopped in his tracks and out of instinct, instantly covered his private parts.

"If you don't take your narrow, black ass in that room and put some clothes on!" She yelled.

King turned quickly and scurried back to his room, embarrassed.

"And tell Candy to bring her fast ass out here!" Suzanne demanded.

"Fuck!" King said as he went back to his room.

Candy had started getting dressed as soon as she heard Suzanne yell at King.

"Damn! My fault baby," he apologized to Candy, who was already operating as fast as lighting. "My mom wants you," King stated. "But give me a second to get dressed." King didn't want her going out to face Suzanne alone, since it was his fault more than hers.

Candy waited for him to dress and they went out to face his mother together.

"Hello Miss Steele," Candy said in a whisper.

"Come on over here and give me a hug child. And I hope you washed your hands." Suzanne joked, making light of the situation.

Candy smirked and took baby steps, fearful of what Suzanne was gonna do. But she only hugged Candy, who was visibly scared, to say the least.

"I'm not upset with you or my hard headed ass son, but I am disappointed. Both of you know better," she said. "I'm really gonna need for both of y'all to make better decisions. Y'all are supposed to be in school. There is nothing in this house for y'all to be skipping school for," she said, starting to get upset. "Ain't no education between that boy's legs either," Suzanne said, pointing at King's mid-section. "And King, you know better! I should take you off of the basketball team."

Threatening to remove him from the team had his bones shaking. "No Ma!" King yelled. "It won't happen again, I promise."

Candy also pleaded for Suzanne not to remove him from the team. They both promised that the situation they were in would never happen again.

"I'm not gonna promise you two nothing," Suzanne told them.

After all the embarrassment they talked with Suzanne for a few minutes and then excused themselves. King took Candy home and then returned to the house. When he came in again, his mom was still sitting in the exact same spot.

At her appointment that morning, the doctor had confirmed that she had breast cancer. She had known that something wasn't right lately, she had been dog tired from doing absolutely nothing. Her co-workers had been telling her that she looked tired and her skin tone was becoming ashen. After talking to several of the girls at work, they prompted her to go get a physical and blood work done.

Suzanne had always taken pride in her appearance and her health. She looked good for 45 and could easily pass for 35 on any given day. Everyone praised her for being beautiful and being in such good health. Women her age usually had one trait or the other, but not usually both.

Three months passed after she first found out that she had breast cancer and the disease had been killing her softly and slowly. King was also feeling repercussions of the disease. He had been missing basketball practice so he could go to chemo therapy with his mom and he had started failing classes from staying up late at night, taking care of his mother.

Eventually, her left breast was removed and she started losing her hair. She had stopped eating and her weight was deteriorating. The doctors had been blunt with her and told her how much time she had left. When they had discovered that she had breast cancer, it was already too late, it had spread throughout her body. The medicine she was prescribed was not helping and the chemotherapy only slowed it down. Suzanne had approximately two weeks to live.

DC had moved into the house with them and stayed by her side throughout her last days. King stayed home from school and together they all stayed close in that one room in West Cliff. They joked about the old days and laughed constantly, none of them shed a tear during those last days. They all stayed strong for each other during this trying time.

Everything seemed to be good until Friday night. Suzanne passed that night, December 1st, 1996. King had never felt a pain like he felt at that moment. His mother had gone to that unknown place, where you either go to Heaven or to Hell. King cried all that night and wouldn't take calls from anyone or see any visitors. DC was running around making all the arrangements and trying to stay busy.

Suzanne's relatives came from all over the country as the next couple days came and went. DC chose to follow her wishes and bury Suzanne beside his mother. It was in her will to have everyone buried beside each another. King received the house and $250,000 in a life insurance, but only after he turned 21.

The day of the funeral the church was packed to capacity. All of her co-workers, Kings basketball coaches and team mates, past and present, and family members that hadn't shown their faces since King was a little boy had showed up to pay respects.

A week after the funeral DC still hadn't left King's side for one minute. They talked and discussed what their futures would be like. King promised that he would continue to get his education and vowed to have everything in life that it had to offer. Whatever wasn't given to him he would take it.

There was a new light burning inside of King and DC had seen it before. It was the same fire that burned inside him when his own mother passed. King would be alright and DC knew that for certain. Anybody that ever crossed King or denied him anything would surely pay for it. There would be hell to pay and the only thing that would stop him was death.

With all the power in him, DC would guide his son to the top. A new King was about to be crowned and DC already had plans to step aside and let King take over. After seeing the look in King's eyes, he knew the time had come.

Chapter 10

Three years later, King was a senior in high school. It 1999 and for the past year Candy and King had been living together. After losing his mother, King had turned into a recluse. Neither DC nor Candy really had any idea how to bring him out of his slump. He wouldn't go to school, he stopped hustling, and he just stopped going outside all together. All King wanted to do was smoke weed and have sex.

Candy was at the point of just boxing everything up and leaving him, but deep down inside she couldn't do it because he needed her. She was mentally drained and her body was wore out physically. She was forced to get on the pill because they were having sex three to four times a day.

All DC could do was be by his son's side, things were taking a toll on him as well. He had suffered a mild stroke a year earlier and it had brought King out of his slump and back to reality. King knew his father needed him and he didn't want to lose all that he had left.

King got up the day after DC's stroke and decided that he was going to put his life back together. With the help of Kareem, DC moved into the house with King. Candy helped King enroll back into school, since King had failed the previous year. He was assigned to 'fast track' so that he could catch up and be placed back in the proper grade. Fast track was a program that allowed students to repeat the grade they failed and also enter into the next grade as well, all in the same year. After completing fast track, the following year the student would be caught up.

DC still conducted business as usual, even though King had taken over all transactions, money laundering and deliveries. To wash their money DC had opened up laundromats, stores, and beauty salons and had taken on all responsibilities of running the legal businesses.

School had become fun again for Candy and King and they were both on schedule to graduate on time. Scouts had starting coming to the house to meet DC and try to get King to commit to their schools. He had already received offers from NC State, Wake Forest, Catawba, Livingstone, Greensboro A&T, and many more. The Division 1 colleges were looking at him because they knew he would be a one year and done player. King had some life changing decisions to make.

Twan was his only comrade out there with him, Revlon and Skinny had been incarcerated. They shot a couple of guys that tried to rob them. They were both scheduled to be released in 16 months. Grinch was still holding the Eastside down with Uncle Len. Uncle Len told King that he had plans on retiring real soon. Len and Candy's mom had become serious. He had popped the question and she accepted. She agreed to marry him if he would leave the drug game alone and he agreed! So Len would be getting married soon.

That left King with some vital decisions to make. Candy was going to college to become a cosmetologist. The beauty salons would be hers in the future, once she and King tied the knot. So it was only right that she learned everything about salons.

"Let's go to the football game tonight," Candy said to King.

"Naw, I can't tonight baby. I got some business to handle," he stated. "Why don't you take Keisha with you and show off your new car," King suggested. He had just bought her a Candy apple red, 1999 Nissan Maxima.

Candy didn't wanna show off the car, she wanted to chill with her man. "I'll just stay here," she said, pouting and stomping into the house.

Uncle Len and King were sitting outside on the porch later when King said, "Look we gotta go to Kannapolis and drop these bricks off."

"I know," Len replied, looking at King with a smirk on his face. "I don't think you're gonna be able to slide."

King just smiled while shaking his head. He never touched the dope as he took his new position as HNIC. They had a routine when it came to transporting dope. Uncle Len would be the lead man, Grinch would be in the middle with the dope in his car, while his girl drove her car behind him. King would bring up the rear so that nobody could get behind Grinch. That's how they would run up and down 85, it never failed.

They had five bricks that were going to a group of thugs in lil Texas, in Kannapolis. King got up and went into the house to kiss Candy and tell her he'd be back shortly.

"Do you know if you'll be back by the time the football game is over?" She questioned.

"Yes, I should be, and I'll take you to Apple Bee's. I know that's where you wanna go," King said, winking at her as he walked out the door. "I love that girl," he said to himself as he got into his car.

They jumped in their cars and drove to the Eastside to meet Grinch and his girl. After that, they would hit the highway. As King drove through the streets, his mind was preoccupied with the play that they were about to go make. He hated dealing with the guys from lil Texas. They were customers from when his father was running things.

When DC was dealing with them he only charged 22k a brick, but since King was taking all the risk, he added on an extra 5k. At first they complained about the increase, but now there was no side talk. The guys went to DC and complained about the extra five grand that had been added on and DC informed them that he was no longer in charge. Either they could deal with King or find a new connect. Things had been running smoothly for the past couple of years, with no more complaints.

When King and Uncle Len pulled up on Shaver Street, Grinch and his girl were on the porch smoking a blunt. Grinch went into the house to lock things up and get ready for the ride. There weren't any pleasantries, everyone was all business.

As they got into their cars you could tell everybody was deep in thought. It would take 20 minutes to get to Kannapolis doing the speed limit. There was to be no smoking anything, no talking on cell phones, or playing loud music while they were in traffic. These were the rules. No exceptions! There could be no reason for anything to jeopardize their goal, or their organization.

Their crew had cautiously been under the radar for years, so they never dealt with any new customers. Anyone that got locked up was immediately bonded out, no matter how much it cost. They were bonded out and had a hired attorney, who had been in DC's pocket before King was born.

There was a stash box placed in all the cars, which cost a pretty penny. King stayed paranoid, even though some wouldn't call it that. They would use, 'being careful'.

As they got to China Grove, which was ten minutes into their trip, traffic had slowed to a snail's pace. Before King could grab his phone it chirped, indicating a message. Looking at the text he saw it was Uncle Len, confirming there was a license check point ahead. King hit back, *"Ok."*

They all had licenses so that wasn't going to be a problem, that's why all drivers involved had to be disciplined. If anyone had been smoking weed and off their game, the whole trip would have been compromised. All because a nigga couldn't wait to smoke.

King smiled knowing he made all the right choices with his people. Everyone had made it through the license check and it was his turn. King pulled up to the check point and rolled his window down.

"License and registration," the officer asked.

King searched through the glove compartment, going through some papers, until he found the registration. As he went to close it, King saw that there was a bag of coke in there as well. He must have forgotten about it because he never rode dirty. He hurried and shut the glove compartment with a loud bang, which startled the officer.

"What's going on?" The officer inquired.

"Nothing sir. It gets stuck at times," King lied.

After looking his license and registration over, the officer looked at King, then back at his license. "Son you look very familiar."

Hearing the offer say that made King nervous and he started sweating profusely as his foot started itching on the accelerator. He looked up and noticed that the crew was moving very slowly in front of him. He sat there nervous as a hotdog in a room with four vicious pit bulls. Then the officer snapped his fingers indicating his thoughts.

"I knew it! I knew it!" He said looking at King. "You're the point guard for Salisbury High School, am I right?" He asked.

"Yes sir," King said, finally able to exhale.

"That's where I recognize you from. You're a helluva player! Officer Cox come over here and meet the next Michael Jordan," he said to the other officer.

Officer Cox came over and extended his hand to King.

"Nice to meet you sir," King said, shaking the officers hand.

"Like wise," Officer Cox replied, looking at him with disdain.

Handing King back his license, the officer said, "I'll see you in a couple of months. Y'all play AL Brown and I'm sure it'll be a good game."

"Yeah, but I doubt it," King said taking his credentials. He pulled off slowly while waving to the officers. Once he was about 100 yards away from them he burst out laughing. He already had it in his mind that they were going have to catch him.

King called Uncle Len as soon as he was back behind Grinch's girl. "The officer knew me from playing basketball," King stated, not believing it himself.

Len chuckled and said that they were approaching the exit. Grinch drove on ahead and went to the store as King followed Grinch and Uncle Len followed King. King called Bandanna, who didn't have to answer, it was the code to let it ring one time then King would hang up, indicating he was at the spot.

Bandanna was in the car wash sitting in a black on black Range Rover with 20's. King parked in the stall next to him and waited patiently for Bandanna to bring him the money. Once Bandanna was in the car and seated, Uncle Len started to wash the car. Grinch and Bandanna talked about the next shipment while King counted the money. He was taught to always count the money, even if it came out of the ATM machine right in front of him.

When Uncle Len was done washing the car, Bandanna got out and went inside the store next to the car wash, while Grinch put the drugs into the Range Rover. If the police came, neither King nor Bandanna were responsible for the drugs. Grinch walked back to King's car as another guy jumped into the Range Rover and pulled off.

Grinch and King pulled off as well, satisfied with how everything went. Grinch's girl sat across the street keeping her eyes open for anything suspicious.

Thirty minutes later they were back on Shaver Street and Grinch's girl had stopped at Apple Bee's where she got everybody something to eat. This was for suspecting eyes that could be watching them. King tried to stay a couple steps ahead of the game.

Chapter 11

Basketball season would be starting in a week and practices had been wearing King down. He was really stressed because this was his senior year and the Scouts would be out real soon. As he left the locker room stuck in his thoughts, he looked outside and noticed Cash talking to Candy, leaning on his car.

"I know this nigga ain't talking to my girl while he's leaning on my shit!" King thought, not believing his eyes. He was furious and each step he took toward them showed it more and more.

Cash saw King approaching and stood straight up, getting off the car. He had a smirk on his face that irked King.

"What's up?" Cash asked, playing it off.

"Y'all tell me," King replied sarcastically.

Cash looked at Candy. "I was asking her where you were because I need to holla at you about something."

"Well next time holla at me when you see me," King said, pointing to himself. "Cause me coming out here seeing you all in my girl's shit while leaning on my car, ain't no good look," King Stated. "That's some real disrespectful shit!" King said, getting upset.

"I respect that," Cash said. "We'll talk about the situation another time," he finished as he walked off leaving King on degrees.

King ignored him and took it for what it was. He got into the passenger seat and remained silent for the twenty minute ride to their house. As King was getting out of the car he slammed his door.

Candy jumped out of reflex. She already knew that King was furious, even though the conversation was meaningless. Being in King's position and his approach to the situation, it would seem fishy. She was slow getting out of the car and entering the house, she felt terrible.

"How are you doing?" DC asked as she came into the living room.

"I'm good," she answered. "Are you taking care of yourself?" She asked.

"One day at a time. What's going on with you and my son?" He questioned, getting up off the couch.

Candy just broke down in tears and told DC about the situation that had just taken place. After hearing the story, DC looked at it as a minor misunderstanding. He saw how King may have took it like that, but it was just a harmless conversation.

"Niggas do indirect shit like that all the time to try and get niggas off their square," DC explained to her. 'A nigga trying to talk to a girl while she's driving another man's car and waiting for that man, was disrespectful. Regardless of what the conversation was about," he said. "Men have become shiesty nowadays. Don't be led into being a pawn in a man's vindictive games," he continued. "King!" DC yelled. "Come downstairs for a minute."

When King got downstairs, DC explained the conversation he just had with Candy.

"Listen Pops. At the end of the day, it was still disrespectful," King said with venom in his eyes. "I feel that she should have told dude to back the fuck up and that I would be out shortly," King fumed.

"Listen son. One thing you will have to learn about females, is they love attention. Point! Blank! Period! She did nothing wrong," DC said.

Hearing this made King feel like his father was taking Candy's side. "Alright Dad, you're right," King agreed. "Now calm down, we don't need your blood pressure rising."

DC felt light headed so he asked Kareem to bring him a bottle of water. King excused himself and went back upstairs with Candy in tow. When they got into the room, Candy sat on the bed and King sat beside her. She was still crying and felt terrible.

Putting his finger underneath her chin, King tilted her head upwards to look at him. "Tell me what he said," King demanded in a soft voice.

She looked him dead in the eyes and repeated what Cash had said, verbatim. "He would love to go out with me but he respected you. Also that he is the real King around here," she said sniffling. "I was gonna tell you soon as you got into the car, but you never gave me the chance," Candy said looking him in the eyes the whole time, as tears slid down her face. "You should know me by now," Candy said. "I belong to you!"

"I believe you baby," King replied, pulling Candy closer to him.

They stared at each other with love in their eyes as he wiped away the tears that were running down her face. He leaned in and kissed her softly with passion as she returned his kisses, which became slower and more sensual.

Then Candy broke their kiss and stood up in front of him. King reached out and pulled her shirt above her head seductively.

After he removed her shirt, Candy took the initiative to do the same to him. She pulled his shirt off and then his pants. King pulled down her pants and she slowly stepped out of them. She sat on the bed and scooted backwards.

Candy had on a red and black lace Victoria Secret bra and panty set. This was King's favorite color, so it aroused him immediately. The panties were see through so you could see her shaved pussy right through the fabric. He stood in his boxers and tank top watching her with the eye of the tiger.

King turned on the radio and a song off Blackstreet's new CD was playing. He turned off the light and walked over to the bed. As he climbed on top of her, he started kissing her eye, then slowly worked his way to her cheeks. Candy took her fingernails and softly moved them up and down his back. Every kiss he put on her made her pussy wetter and her clit throb harder. They kissed as he unsnapped her bra and flung it backwards over his head. Taking her left nipple in his mouth, he set Candy on fire. Kissing and rubbing her areola sent a shock wave between her legs.

King knew how to seduce her and after feeling her shake like a Tsunami, he had to give her what she craved. While he slid out of his boxers, King stuck his fingers into her mouth, allowing her to taste her own juices. She loved when he did that.

"Mmm," she moaned, tasting herself. She wanted to share it with King. Candy pulled him on top of her. She was so wet that he slid right into her. He slid into her tunnel so smooth that it felt like silk.

With every thrust Candy moaned and threw it back. They went thrust for thrust and King slid up and down inside of her like she was made of baby oil. She was in complete ecstasy and he knew that he loved her as her body reacted to his. He felt like he was in Heaven when he was inside of her.

Candy was about to cum and as the first climax came she squirted all over King's dick. He knew that she had squirted because she held him and shook as if her life depended on it. As she came down out of the cloud from her climax she flipped him off of her and started sucking his dick.

King was close to busting his nut, but he wasn't ready to explode yet, so he pulled her up to ride him. She started off like she was on a bull, she squatted down on him and bucked, going fast and then slow.

"Damn bae I'm about to cum!" King yelled through clenched teeth. He grabbed her hips and started banging her harder.

"Mm oh!! Shit!" Candy moaned and grabbed him by the neck, applying pressure.

King pounded harder as she choked him. "Holla out now bitch!" He yelled, slamming his dick in her so hard that she became hoarse.

"Damn! I'm bouta squirt! Oh I'm bouta squirt all on this dick!" Candy stammered.

"Make that pussy spit!" King demanded.

"I'm, oh..., I'm spi... tting baby," Candy mumbled as King dug deeper. She squirted like a pipe had just busted and it brought him closer to climax.

Every time she came down on him, cum splashed against him and all over his chest. Her juices were all on his face. "Damn you bouta catch this one!" King yelled while he deep stroked. "Bae..., oh Bae..., catch this..., oh! Shit!" King stuttered as he got ready to erupt.

Before he could say another word, Candy hoped off his dick just in time to catch his load in her mouth.

"Motherfu—er!" King yelled while grabbing the back of Candy's head, forcing his dick down her throat. "Swallow that shit!" He continued talking shit while humping her face. "Damn I love you girl!" He insisted.

He made sure she got the last few drops as he played with her hair. He thought about all the good times they shared. All the times she had shown him that she loved and cherished him and worshiped the ground that he walked on.

Rolling over and lying beside him, Candy kissed King deeply. She opened her eyes and looked at him to find he was smiling like the cat that ate the canary.

"What are you smiling about?" She asked.

"Love is a beautiful thing," he replied.

They started kissing passionately again and round two began.

Chapter 12

"This shit is gonna have niggas with lock jaw," Cash said to himself as he wiped up the cocaine in the Pyrex. *"Damn, I almost had Candy until King's punk ass came out,"* he thought to himself. "Oh shit! There's a basketball game tonight. Is it in Kannapolis?" Cash asked his homeboy Redrum, who was sitting in the corner, smoking a blunt.

"Yeah, it is," Redrum replied.

"I'm with it. I'm bout done with this shit. It'll be dry in about two minutes, then we gotta take it to Smoke over on the Eastside," Cash stated.

He knew that King and all the NAAM niggas would be getting ready to head to the game. When King had a game there was so much money to be made. All his crew members were sure to be at his games, no matter where they were. Nobody hustled on the days he played, it was like a holiday or some shit. All the other hustlers took advantage of those days.

Cash had whipped up 4 ½ ounces to take to Smoke. Smoke didn't fuck with King or his crew, he still harbored feelings towards King because Candy didn't give him no play. So he took his money to anybody besides King.

Cash looked at his watch to check the time when Redrum broke his concentration. "Yo! Your phone ringing," Redrum stated.

He picked his phone up off the table in the living room and answered, "What's good?" A minute later he said, "Ok. I'll be there in 15 minutes." Cash hung up, then made sure things were put up in the room. When they were satisfied that everything was put away, Cash and Redrum headed out the door.

"Let's get this money," Cash said as he rubbed his hands together. He was driving a Delta 88 on 20's. It was painted cherry red with peanut butter seats. Everything on the inside was woodgrain, the dash board included. He had the loudest sound system to be heard in Salisbury. You were sure to hear him way before you saw him.

As they rode in silence, Cash told Redrum about how he almost had Candy.

"Ain't that King's bitch?" Redrum asked, not feeling where the conversation was going.

For now, Cash replied with a smirk on his face. Redrum tried to laugh it off until he noticed the stern look on Cash's face. He didn't want any bad dealings with King, he knew all about the moves King was making. Everybody knew that the young Eastside boys were killers. He had seen it firsthand himself not long ago. He replayed in his mind when they were on the Westside one day. There was a lil nigga there that owed Twan some money, named Pop. The nigga had been telling people that he ain't paying them Eastside niggas shit. Pop had been ducking Twan for almost two months. To make matters worse, he had the money to pay him.

They were at Texaco when Twan and Skinny pulled up. Pop was inside the store with his crew. Skinny walked in, spotted Pop and acted as if he didn't see him or his crew. Ironically, Pop was telling one of his people that Twan had called him and he told Twan to suck his dick and hung up on him.

When Skinny heard him say that, he wanted to see where this nigga's heart was at! "Is that right?" Skinny asked, walking up behind him.

Not recognizing his voice, Pop turned around and saw Skinny. Pop stood about 6'2" and weighed in at 225 pounds, with brown skin. All the blood had completely drained from his face when he realized that Skinny had heard the whole conversation. He didn't have a choice but to keep up the macho façade, but his mouth had gotten dryer than the desert after no rain for months.

"Uh! Yeah! You heard what I said!" Pop barked, shaking like Muhammad Ali.

Skinny smiled and threw his hands up in surrender. Seeing as though Skinny had showed a sign of weakness by throwing his hands up, Pop did exactly what Skinny wanted. He started adding insult to injury and adding fuel to the situation.

"Yeah! I told that mother fucker he could suck my dick!" Pop repeated, this time with more of the antics and swag of a real killer.

Since Skinny had shown up his boys were really gassing him up now. "You heard what my nigga said. Fuck Twan!" One of the guys said.

Skinny kept right on laughing as though he was at a comedy show. He had his gun on him and his trigger finger was itching to bust these niggas. As Skinny got to the counter he threw a $20 bill on it and walked out. Pop and his boys had already left out the door in front of him and he didn't even wait on his change.

Once outside the store there was so many people that Twan couldn't see Skinny in the crowd. Skinny yelled, "Aye Pop!" Out loud so Twan could hear him.

Twan thought he was trippin when he heard someone call Pop's name, but he looked up instantly.

Skinny continued, "Is there anything you want me to tell my nigga Twan?"

After hearing the exchange between the two men Twan was suspicious. He started creeping closer and heard, "Fuck it! I'ma say it one more time," Pop said, grand standing. A crowd had gathered to see what was happening and Pop couldn't help but degrade Twan again in front of his crew and other niggas that were there. "Tell-Twan-I-Said-Suck-My-...,"

Before he could get the last part out, Twan came from between two cars so fast he was just a streak and stuck the barrel of a .40 cal. in Pop's mouth. Everything slowed down as if time had frozen.

"Bang!" Twan blew Pop's shit backwards and all over his homeboy's face, right in front of everybody.

Skinny already had his shit out. Bang! Bang! Bang! He shot the closest two guys to Pop. As they tried to draw their weapons it was already too late he had the drop on them. It was a massacre and nobody said shit.

"I don't give a fuck about that shit!" Cash yelled after hearing the story.

"I was just saying that I don't think you should fuck with King's girl," Redrum stuttered.

Cash couldn't believe the shit he was hearing. His gun play was just as vicious as anybody else's. Cash had a couple bodies under his belt to go along with a couple of shootings. He wasn't no slouch and Redrum knew it.

Cash pulled his car over on the side of the road by Lincoln Apartments. They were on the Eastside.

"What's going on?" Redrum asked, looking around suspiciously.

"There's an ambulance coming down the street," Cash replied with a sinister grin on his face.

"Where?" Redrum asked, damn near turning his head around to look out the car. "I don't see them."

"Get the fuck out my car!" Cash screamed. "Since you so God damn scared of King!"

Seeing Cash mad made Redrum grab the door handle and step out of the car. When his second foot hit the pavement, Cash shot him in the ass and then peeled out, leaving him holding his ass on the ground, flopping like a fish out of water.

Cash drove off laughing hysterically and looking in the rearview mirror. Redrum was beyond mad.

Smoke was at the store when Cash pulled up. He pulled into the parking lot like a bat outta hell. Smoke was about to take flight until he saw Cash laughing like hell. Cash got out of the car comical as hell.

"What's up?" Smoke asked, ready to cap and go.

"Ain't nothing man! Here you go," Cash said handing Smoke a black bag with the drugs inside. He kept walking and went into the store.

Smoke went to the car and started counting the money. Once Cash got back in the car, he asked Smoke if he was going to the game.

"Naw, I'm gonna stay here and grind since everybody is at the game," Smoke answered.

Cash said, "Cool."

Smoke got out of the car, leaving the money in the seat.

Cash counted the money and got on the highway, headed to the basketball game.

This was the third game of the season and King had waited for this moment all year long. He saw the officer from the license check point. The officer gave King a head nod, acknowledging him and King did the same in response. They spoke briefly, but King felt uncomfortable talking to the police per se.

All of his homies were there to see him put on and the Scouts and Recruiters were in attendance as well. There were even some NBA veterans there. King scored 15 points in his first game and 21 points in his second game. Kannapolis was also undefeated. They had a point guard that was a prospect to go to college for one year, then to the NBA. This game was a test for King and his squad.

Candy sat in the second row, across from the player's bench. She wanted King to see her at every move and assure him that she was there for him and only him! She had two of her home girls with her.

The game was about to commence as they started announcing the starting line-up for both teams. King was more hyper than usual, he knew he had something to prove tonight. The introductions ended and both teams took the floor. Kannapolis won the tip off and went to score the first two points. They went at it basket for basket in the first two quarters. At the half, Kannapolis was up by one point.

King had a season high at the half, 15 points, and 8 assists with 3 rebounds. During the shoot around, King noticed that Cash had come and sat in the row behind Candy. He brushed it off because he knew that Candy was loyal.

Cash looked at King and pointed at the score board as if mocking him. King smiled, knowing what Cash was up to. The buzzer sounded and then both teams ran to their benches. While in the huddle, King told his team mates to turn it up a notch. All the players smiled, put their hands in the middle and then yelled at the same time "turn-up!"

"I got the point guard, Randal," King told the coach, then ran onto the court. King wanted to prove to the scouts, the recruits, and to himself, that he was better than Randal on both sides of the ball, offence and defense.

Salisbury got the ball to start the second half, the score was 42 to 41 Kannapolis' way. King's home boy came down and passed him the ball. King crossed over one player and drove to the basket. As he drove, he bounce passed the ball to Eaman, cutting on the baseline for the dunk.

The crowd went crazy and King back pedaled to find Randal, who was coming to receive the ball. He found his man and stuck to him, like shit on toilet paper. King had clamps on Randal for the rest of the game, he couldn't do anything without King being there.

After it was all said and done, King had an astounding 37 points, 13 assists, 6 rebounds, and 8 steals. Salisbury had won 75 to 63. Randal was shut down and King showed the scouts he was the better player between the two.

Candy came over and hugged King at the end of the game. Cash was getting up to leave with the rest of the crowd when King stopped him and pointed at the scoreboard. Cash looked back at King and then at Candy with a smirk on his face. King kissed Candy then told her he would meet her outside. He spoke to her friends who looked at him with lust in their eyes as he jogged off.

King's homies each came up to him and showered him with hugs and pounds. From the outside looking in, you would have thought he was a movie star. He ran into the locker room to shower and he came out to the parking lot it was still jammed packed. All the East siders were outside their cars with the music blasting, smoking weed.

Twan had the loudest system and all you could hear was everyone singing, "Ripping and Running" by BoodaMan! It was their anthem and they hustled to it on a regular basis. King put his gym bag into the car Candy was sitting on and joined the party.

While everyone was celebrating, Cash pulled up and got out of his car. He was the only nigga from the Westside at the game. He slowly walked up to King, putting everybody on edge, sensing that there was about to be an altercation.

King walked around the car to see what Cash had to say. Once they were face to face, Cash extended his hand and told King that he played a good game. Hearing this made King relax a little bit.

"Thanks!" King said, shaking hands with him.

"You seemed worried when I sat behind your girl," Cash stated, surprising King.

That was some slick shit King hadn't expected him to say. King was a hustler by nature, but he was also a thinker. Cash was trying to distract him by sitting behind Candy and King had been on it already.

"Wow! I wasn't worried about you sitting by my Queen," King stated nonchalantly. "I know when I got one she's mine."

Cash looked over at Candy chilling with her home girls, then he looked back at King. "You better hold onto her. Everybody gets a sweet tooth every now and then," he taunted.

"I feel you on that," King said, looking Cash directly in his eyes. "But once you get a sweet tooth, I'll be the one to pull your teeth," King stated in a murderous tone.

Cash walked off, knowing that he had made the first move.

King turned away and went back to celebrating his victory with his homies. In his mind he knew that a war had just been started. King knew that Cash tried to make it about Candy, but he knew that it was bigger than that. What just took place was the first rule of engagement.

Chapter 13

The basketball season had been going well and Salisbury High School was in first place in their conference. It was December 5th and the Christmas tournament was fast approaching. DC and King were scheduled to visit NC State the coming weekend.

Candy had also received a scholarship to attend NC State, she was planning on working towards a degree in accounting. She and King had discussed their options, they would choose between NC State and Wake Forest. Candy's scholarship was for NC State, but if they decided on Wake Forest it wouldn't be an issue because money was not a problem. King had already stated that he would pay her intuition.

King, DC, and Candy were all excited about their trip to NC State.

"I want to tell you guys how proud I am of both of you," DC stated. "It's good to have an education in the world we live in today. Money is good, but with an education, a lot of doors may be opened."

"Thanks Dad," King replied.

King knew that his father's health hadn't been its best lately. They had talked recently and DC stated that he was going to get all the way out of the game, even leaving the legal business to King eventually. That's why King decided to major in business. The

NBA was definitely in his future, but school would remain a top priority in the off season.

As they traveled up highway 85, Candy sat looking out the window, caught up in her own thoughts of when King went to the NBA. She would be stuck in Raleigh or Winston-Salem. There were gonna be all types of women at King's disposal. Not like the chicken heads floating around Salisbury, but exotic video vixens and American top models. She wasn't worried about the local chicks, she knew none of them could take her crown. Candy trusted King because he had never cheated on her. He also had always had money, so that wouldn't change him.

She looked up and King was staring her dead in the eyes. He could sense that something was bothering her.

"What is it?" King asked while squeezing her hand gently.

"Just thinking," she replied. "It's just amazing how time flies. It seems like just yesterday we were freshmen in high school and now, today, we're seniors visiting colleges to become freshmen again," she said giggling.

"Yes. We are moving forward in life," King said as Candy took a deep breath and looked out the window. "I've noticed that you seem to have a lot on your mind lately," King said.

Candy just looked at him lovingly.

"I wanna reassure you that when I go to the NBA, you will be with me every weekend no matter where I am. I will not change baby!" He assured her. "You are everything to me and I never thought that someone could be everything to somebody." King was confessing his love for her and giving her plenty of pennies for her thoughts.

Candy was elated to hear the things that King was saying to her. At the moment, it was a weight being lifted from her shoulders.

They had been on the highway for almost two hours and would reach their destination in the next thirty minutes. After stopping to get gas and something to eat, they had arrived.

As they were parking DC stated, "Today is gonna be a great day!"

Kareem nodded his head, agreeing with his friend.

As they walked the walkway, they saw a campus guide in front of the administration building holding a sign that said Cummings Family. DC thought that it was hospitable that they would arrange such greetings.

The group walked to the guide and exchanged pleasantries. The guide was a curvaceous female whose name tag read Timiya. She was a thick red bone that stood about 5'5" and had slanted eyes. She also had a body that would shame a Coca-Cola bottle.

Candy looked at King, who had a smirk on his face. DC was also looking at King and watching Timiya.

"Right this way lady and gentlemen," Timiya said wanting them to follow her.

As they walked around campus Timiya gave King the tour as if there wasn't anyone else there. She seemed like she really wanted him to come to that school.

DC asked questions about any rapes, or missing females reported in the area, and if so, how many? Timiya didn't have any of those statistics, but assured them that she would have those answers before they departed.

King asked to be taken to the gymnasium to meet with the coaching staff and when they arrived, the head coach and his assistant were there waiting.

Timiya grabbed Candy's hand to resume the tour as if they were long lost friends. She thought it was best that the men talk, since King was the reason for the tour.

"Welcome Mr. Carter and King! We are so glad to have you explore our campus as one of your options. Here at State we take pride in our students. Education has always been our top priority and athleticism comes second," Coach Jones informed them. "We plan on you being our starting point guard and we're interested in knowing the type of offense you like to run?"

King was caught off guard with that question, he didn't know how to answer. It really was a trick question, because if he didn't attend State, they could use his answer against him.

"Well, I'm a diverse player who can adjust to any offense against any defense," King said with pride.

DC was very pleased with his answer and how he thought about it before he said it.

"I like that answer," Coach Jones said as they walked the hallways, headed to the weight room.

King felt like the interview was going quite well and he had showed his father that he could handle dealing with different people, on many different levels. King was a hustler by nature, with a gift for gab. He seemed to be in his element, even when he stepped outside his boundaries.

DC had to admit that his son was indeed diverse, he had handled the day like a pro.

Once inside the weight room, King met some of the players that he could potentially be playing with. They chatted about all the things they heard about him, mostly about the tapes they had watched with Coach Jones. He was receptive to the comments and attention that came from the players and had a good time.

Later, he met Timiya and Candy at the school's cafeteria for lunch. When they got there, Coach Jones had everyone escorted to the conference room. There were Philly cheesesteak subs, French fries and iced tea in abundance on the table.

Timiya was asked to attend as well and they all sat down to eat lunch and talk about the experience. Timiya had also gotten the answers to all of DC's questions.

King kept glancing at Timiya seductively as she talked and Candy had caught him eyeing her a couple of times. He would turn his head as if he wasn't paying attention.

"So what do you think of our campus?" Coach Jones asked.

Caught up in his thoughts of Timiya, King didn't answer immediately.

"So, do you think you would be interested in attending State?" DC asked.

Trying to avoid an altercation, this time King took Candy by the hand and squeezed it to get some kind of confirmation. She didn't respond so King responded on his own.

"Well," King said with a long pause. He looked at Candy, who gave him a nod. "Well," King repeated. "I really enjoyed the tour, honestly I did. I liked the fact that no rapes have been committed this year. Also I 'm thankful that racism and discrimination doesn't have value at this school and the crime rate is down 10% in the last two years. Also, I think that the guys on the team accepted me and what I can bring to the team," King explained. He really liked the school but wanted to talk to Candy first. "May I think about it and get back with you Coach Jones?" He asked.

"Of course you can," Coach Jones answered slowly. He was hoping King would commit, at least verbally, today. That wasn't the norm though, signing day was a few months away. Coach Jones was trying to take King off the market and he knew it.

They finished eating and were all escorted back to the front of the administration building.

"It was a pleasure meeting you Mr. Carter," Coach Jones said extending his hand.

"The pleasure was all mine," DC said, returning the gesture.

"Well King, I hope you're considering coming to State. We look forward to seeing you in the fall," Coach Jones said with a Kool-Aid smile on his face.

"Thank you Coach," King said, shaking his hand. "Also, I would like to thank you for the tour," King said shaking Timiya's hand.

Timiya slid King her number on the sly, while shaking his hand. "Hope to see you in the fall," she said, embracing Candy.

Candy embraced her back while they talked about calling one another.

King got back in the jeep with his mind clouded.

Chapter 14

"Christmas Eve is tomorrow," King said to Candy. "What's on the menu for Christmas dinner?"

"Well I was hoping we could just eat at my mom's house and invite your father," Candy said.

"That sounds like a very good idea," King replied. "I'll call him and see if he has any plans."

"What do you think about NC State?" Candy inquired.

"I told you from the beginning that I would let you decide," he reminded her.

They had discussed their decision on many occasions and King had given her the same answer every time she asked. He didn't want to say NC State, because of how she caught him looking at Timiya. Wake Forest was an option because he was thinking about expanding his drug operation into Winston-Salem. Either way the decision was Candy's to make.

"Baby I don't wanna have his conversation every day, so I need you to give me and answer today," King stated with emphasis. He was ready to commit to a school so his thoughts were clear and he could move on with his life.

After every basketball game the first question by the reporters would always be, "*Where do you plan on going to college next year?"* The repetitive question was causing him irritation and frustration.

Candy had already made her mind up, she had her answer a couple of days after the visit at NC State. She and Timiya had been talking on the phone every day since the tour and as they talked, Timiya made it clear, on numerous occasions that she was bisexual. She admitted that she was interested in King, but after seeing Candy, she had an attraction to both of them. Candy advised Timiya that she was strictly dickly and that she would appreciate if she respect she and Kings relationship. Timiya agreed and said that she still wanted both of them to come to State. Candy was skeptical at first, but she had already made up her mind, NC State would be the next step in moving forward with their future.

"Ok! I've finally decided that we will attend NC State," she said with certainty. She paused for a brief moment to let her answer sink in and tried to gauge Kings reaction.

He sat there emotionless as possible, but on the inside he was doing backflips. "Is that your final answer?" He asked nonchalantly.

Candy didn't know what to say at the moment. He questioned her as though her answer wasn't what he wanted to hear. "Yes, that is my final answer baby."

King got up from the table and kissed her on the forehead. "I have to call my father and inform him of our decision. Also, I have to see about his plans for Christmas dinner," King said as he walked off.

He was ecstatic about her decision, now he could have peace of mind. He had a basketball game tomorrow and the reporters were bound to ask him the reoccurring question. Finally he could give them the answer to their question, but not the school!

As King was about to call his father, there was a knock at the door. After grabbing his gun from the compartment that was built into the hallway, he looked on the monitor and saw it was Uncle Len. King opened the door and Len came through, followed by two masked men who had their pistols pointed at the back of Len's head. As they pushed their way in, one pointed a gun at King, who had just noticed that Len's face was bloody and his front teeth had been knocked out.

"Back the fuck up!" One of the masked men said to King.

He backed up as he was told.

"Give me the pistol slowly, or I'ma shoot this old bastard."

King reluctantly gave the man the pistol.

"Is there anyone else in the house?" The gunman asked.

"Yes, Candy!" King yelled her name. "Candy could you come here baby?" King yelled again so she would come immediately. King prayed that nobody would get hurt.

Candy came around the corner and froze like she had cement shoes on. The scene in front of her wasn't what she expected to see.

"Come over here," King coaxed her.

Visibly shaken, she did as he asked her. King was trying to see if he could recognize anything familiar about the men. Their voice, walk, or body types. Nothing jumped out at him.

"No one will be hurt if you comply with our demands."

King never thought this day would come but he had planned for it. "I'll give you what you want," King assured them. "Go upstairs to the second room on the right. Once you enter the room, go pull up the carpet that's to your right," King explained. "When you lift the carpet you will see a safe built into the floor. The code is 22-20-4-3. Inside is a brick of cocaine and $100,000 cash. That's all that I have," he confessed. "I don't have anything else here."

"If what you say is upstairs, then we'll be on our way," the masked gunman stated. "Go upstairs and check," he told his partner as he held the gun to King.

Uncle Len stretched out on the couch in severe pain and while his partner was upstairs, the gunman turned the gun on Len. "Now, was that so hard Len?" He asked.

Uncle Len did not respond to the man. The gunman must have gotten upset that Len didn't respond because he walked over to the couch and smacked the hell out of Len. "Whack!"

"Arggg!" Len yelled as he fell off the couch onto his hands and knees.

"There was no need for that!" Candy yelled at the gunman.

King could hear the man upstairs rambling though his belongings.

"Shut up bitch!" The gunmen yelled, pointing his gun at Candy.

King pulled her behind him, shielding her from any harm.

Everyone turned around when they heard the other gunmen coming down the stairs with a pillowcase filled with something. "I got it brah," he said to his commander. "Let's be out."

"What are we gonna do about him?" The shorter one asked, pointing at Len.

"Fuck'em! His old ass know how to stay in his place! Ain't that right?" The taller one said.

Len mumbled something that couldn't nobody understand, his lips were swollen to the size of overheated hotdogs.

Instantly, the taller one started beating Len senseless with the gun.

"Stop!" King demanded. "You got what the fuck you came for, now get the fuck out my house!"

The gunmen backed up abruptly with the gun trained on King the whole time. As they neared the door, the shorter one fired at them and turned to run. The shot didn't hit anybody luckily.

When they had fled from the house Candy ran to get her phone to call the ambulance. King snatched the phone from her and yelled, "Get the car keys!"

Candy sprinted into the kitchen to get the car keys. King didn't want the police coming to his house. Once they saw how bad Uncle Len was beaten, they would have been suspicious. Their first thoughts would have been that it was a robbery. King didn't want that kind of heat, or need it furthermore.

"Come help me," she said, snapping him out of his thoughts.

She had come to help King lift Uncle Len. It wasn't looking good for him. They wobbled to the front door and stood there while she went to get the car. Seconds later she drove on the lawn with no remorse to pull the car up to the front door.

Len was able to assist King with getting inside the car. Once in the car, Len stretched across the backseat. King ran around and jumped into the passenger seat and ten minutes later, after running red lights and stop signs, they arrived at the hospital.

Candy slid to a stop in front of the emergency room and laid on the horn. EMT workers spilled out of the hospital in a frenzy. King helped them get Len out of the backseat and strap him to a gurney.

After telling them what happened and filling out the paperwork, King called his father to come to the hospital. Candy had gone to park the car and as she was returning, she bumped into DC and Kareem. When they got into the waiting area Twan came in and greeted them.

King got up and hugged his father as Candy came in and stood beside King as they huddled by the entrance, whispering in hushed tones.

"How is he?" DC asked nervously.

"They haven't been back out here since they took him in the back," King replied. "He was pretty bad from my observation, but he should be all right," King assured his father confidently.

"What happened?" Twan asked, ready to find the culprits that were responsible.

King gave them the rundown from the time Len knocked on the door to getting to the hospital. "Before that I don't know what led them to my house," King admitted.

"Mr. Carter?" The nurse said seeing DC.

He turned and walked to meet the nurse at the front desk with everyone following right behind. They all stood in front of the nurse, waiting on the results.

"Mr. Carter, your brother is going to be all right," the nurse stated. "He sustained four broken ribs, a bruised spinal cord, a concussion, and a few bruises and lacerations. We'll have to keep him for a few days of course, to keep an eye on the swelling and inflammation."

"Thank you very much," DC said, shaking the woman's hand. "Also, I have his insurance cards with me to complete his paperwork," he informed the nurse.

Just as they were about to leave, Candy's mom came through the door with her eyes bloodshot and swollen. She had her

Walmart vest on so she must have just gotten off work. She ran straight into Candy's waiting arms.

"How is he?" She asked while sobbing uncontrollably.

"Come on," Candy said, leading her to the receptionist to get Len's room number. She came back and informed King that she was going to stay at the hospital with her mom. "I'll call you when I'm ready," she told him. She kissed him and ran back to be with her mom.

When the men walked out of the hospital, Kareem asked King, "Could you tell who the men were?"

"I didn't notice anything distinguishable about either man," King said.

Twan was fuming. "Damn!" He said, punching his fist into the palm of his hand. "Somebody gotta pay!" Twan said angrily.

"Guess what," King said smiling.

"What?" They all yelled in unison, hoping King had found something to go on. "These niggas gonna be mad at me," King said, laughing hysterically.

"What makes you say that?" Twan asked with a smirk on his face.

"I told them I had a brick of cocaine and $100,000 in the safe."

"Ok, well?" DC questioned, looking puzzled.

"It was a brick," King said, making air quotes. "But it was a brick of baking soda and goodie powder and the $100,000 was really $10,000."

Everyone burst out laughing.

"I put a couple hundred dollar bills on top of each stack and in between was all dollar bills," King said laughing hysterically.

Hearing his revolution let DC know that King was officially ready for the world.

Once all the laughter had died down, King got his dad's attention. "Oh! Dad! By the way, I have decided that I'm gonna go to NC State."

DC Looked at his son and put his hand on his shoulder. "I figured that you would. That tour guide influenced your decision didn't she?" DC inquired.

She really did but he wouldn't let his father know that. "No! Not at all," King lied. "I left the decision up to Candy and she chose State."

"I'll take care of this problem we had tonight and you get ready for signing day," DC stated.

Twan looked on in admiration as he wrestled with his own thoughts. Twan was gonna kill the guy responsible for coming into King's house. It was time to lay down the law, masks were coming off!!

King was about to be making more money than they had ever seen. Niggas had to know that King and the NAAM niggas were not to be fucked with.

Chapter 15

Christmas had come and gone like a thief in the night. Uncle Len had recovered from his wounds, but still had scars. He moved Candy's mom out of the hood and into a nice three-bedroom house in a safe cul-de-sac on the outskirts of Salisbury.

King and Len decided that his altercation was a sign for him to go into retirement. It was King's idea, but DC reinforced it. Len really wasn't opposed to the decision that was made. He wanted to marry Candy's mom, Lauren, and being in the game was stopping him from doing that.

Salisbury High won the Christmas tournament and after one of the games, King was seen talking to Coach Jones. That wasn't good thinking on either of their behalf's. Players were not allowed to interact with coaches or scouts at any time while they were still considered a student in high school.

It was New Year's Eve and King was on his way to pick up Candy from a friend's house, they were about to go party in Charlotte. *"This is going to be the best New Year's ever,"* King thought to himself. Months ago he had reserved a suite at the Wingate Motel for the weekend. Twan and his girl were supposed to meet them there.

When King pulled up to April's house Candy was already outside, waiting patiently.

"Hey baby!" Candy called out, getting into the car and kissing King. "I didn't know who you were pulling into the driveway," she stated.

King had bought a new S 500 Benz for Christmas, but never drove it. The car was pearl white with his name embroidered in the driver's headrest. Also, the interior was cocaine white, with LED lights inside and the headlights were also LED. The dashboard and everything else on the inside was wood grain, but the main attraction was the 24 inch TV mounted on the ceiling, with a 15 inch pop out in the console. The car was lean, mean and clean.

King laughed at her comment. "Are you ready for tonight?" He asked.

"I'm ready to party like there's no tomorrow," Candy replied, turning up the music.

As King drove, Candy danced in her seat, more hyper than she would normally be. Maybe she needed this night out more than he thought. King had noticed that she had been tense the past few days.

King reached over and turn the radio down. "Are you all right?" King asked, looking at her with a serious stare.

Candy stared back at him, thinking about his question. "Baby I'm good! I'm just happy that we are together and alive to see another year come in. The night before Christmas really made me think about life," she confessed. "I could have lost you that night and it constantly replays in the back of my mind," she explained.

King replayed the night in question in his own mind as he drove, gripping the steering wheel tighter. They had moved into another house since then, but their belongings were still at the old house. DC had pulled some strings and had them into a house the next day, just in case the gunman came back another time. Nobody knew that they had moved, not even Twan, and they were going to try and keep it like that.

King pulled into the driveway of their new house in Cleveland. He turned off the car and looked deep into Candy's eyes. "Listen to me baby," he said with love in his eyes. "I will never let anything happen to you, or let anybody hurt you. What happened on Christmas Eve was bound to happen sooner or later. I never doubted that it would happen. That's why I had planned ahead," he admitted. "I gave them fake dope and $10,000 in ones. They weren't gonna kill us that night."

As King tried to continue, Candy blurted out, "How do you know?"

King replied, "Because they had on masks."

She just sat there, not understanding what she had just heard.

"If they were coming there to kill us baby, they wouldn't have taken the time to put on masks," King explained.

Candy grabbed King's hand as they sat in the car facing each other. "I trust you and the choices you make," Candy said. "But I don't ever want to be put in that position again. Can you promise me that won't ever happen again?" She questioned with pleading eyes. She hoped that he could.

King never lied to her intentionally. He sat there at that time and really had to think about her question before speaking. Honestly, the only way for him not to allow her or him to be put in that position, was to quit hustling. But even that wasn't a guarantee, they could always try him again. So, to be honest with her, he told the truth.

"Baby I can't say that we will never be put in that position again," King said as he held her hands gently and looked into her tear stained face. "I can promise you that I will make better decisions and be more prepared than last time. Also, I can promise you that I am going to find out who it was and kill them," King said calmly. "Do you trust me?" He asked.

"Yes, Baby. I trust you. I trust you with my life," Candy assured him.

"Well, don't worry about anything then. Just focus on your career and score. I got this," King stated confidently. "Now come on, so we can get dressed and party like rock stars," King said, kissing her before they exited the car.

The couple went into their new, fully furnished house, to prepare for the night out. King felt bad about Christmas Eve, but he had put a reward out for the masked men that busted into his house. Uncle Len knew who the men were, but he didn't know their names. He vowed that if he ever saw them again, he would kill them where they stood and King believed him too!

DC had rewards out as well, so whoever the culprits were, their time was limited. They would definitely be caught soon.

Soon as Candy got out of the shower, King jumped in. *"Damn! I should get me a quickie,"* King thought. Candy had just passed him with water glistening all over her body. King massaged himself while looking at her as she dried off. She must have felt his eyes on her because she turned around seductively and spread her legs wide open. King watched from the shower as Candy danced to music in her head. Slowly, she traced a finger down to her love tunnel, then stuck her finger inside herself real deep. When she pulled it out, there were secretions dripping from her finger like honey. Slowly, she inserted her finger into her mouth, as if she were sucking King's dick. In and out, she sucked sexily.

King had to get out of the shower so they wouldn't be late. Candy was on the other side of the door, moaning loudly. *"She's trying the hell out of me."* King thought as he hurried to wash himself.

When he stepped into the bedroom she was completely dressed. He was dripping wet and sexually frustrated. "That was quite a show you put on," he said, stepping around Candy.

"I'm sorry baby, I really had to get me one before we went out," she stated, smiling mischievously.

"You know I would need at least 45 minutes." he commented, putting on his boxers.

Thirty minutes later, they were both finally dress to impress.

"Let's go," King said, walking out the front door at a brisk pace.

To say they were dressed to impress was an understatement. King had on an all-black Versace linen pants set. The shirt was black and gold, short sleeved. He also had on a gold Cuban link necklace, with a gold matching bracelet. His loafers were black with a gold V on them, representing Versace, and no socks! He looked as if he were going to a GQ photo shoot.

Candy had on an all-black, lace, see-through, Versace dress, that came above her knees. She was drenched in diamonds with thigh, high heeled Versace boots that had strings wrapped around her calves. She also had a V on the front of her boots. They were killing their outfits and they knew it.

King had called Twan to inform them that they were on their way to the motel. Twan was already in Concord, eating, so they didn't have to rush. It would take King almost thirty minutes to get there.

He and Candy discussed school and basketball as they rode, anticipating their night out. When they arrived at the motel, King grabbed their luggage out of the car and Candy was already at the reception desk, checking in.

When they got to their room, Twan was already calling King's phone to see what room they were in. As they got settled in, there was a knock at the door. Twan and his date, Shonda, had arrived. They all settled in and sat in the room taking shots and smoking a blunt before heading out.

"We partying all night!" Twan exclaimed, he was hyped.

"Let me show you around the suite," King insisted.

The young men walked and talked as King showed him around. "Have you heard anything about Christmas Eve?" King asked.

"Nigga's is tightlipped right now, but I'm sure it won't be much longer before we hear something," Twan replied.

"We're gonna get to the bottom of this," King said, putting his hand on Twan's shoulder. "Brah, Candy is traumatized because of what happened. I can't ever let that shit happen again," King confessed.

"I feel ya," Twan agreed, looking him dead in the eyes.

"Can you guys come on?" Candy shouted from the living room.

"OK! OK! Let's go," King said, coming into the room followed by Twan.

"We're riding with y'all," Twan stated.

As soon as they all got into the car, Twan fired up half a blunt of dro. Noone was allowed to smoke in King's car, but he made an exception for Twan. He didn't complain or ask him to put it out.

It took them twenty minutes to get to Sugar Creek in Charlotte. Their destination to bring in the New Year was The Tunnel. It was a hip-hop, mixed crowd. There was always violence and altercations at every club and The Tunnel was no exception.

They had already made plans to stay and party until 1 am, hopefully the ladies would be drunk and tired of dancing by then.

"This place is jam packed," Shonda said as King cruised through rows and rows of cars, trying to find a parking space.

After fifteen minutes of trying to find a spot, they finally succeeded. When they stepped out of the car onlookers were ogling the group as if they were celebrities. The S 500 Benz had just been detailed so it looked like it just came off the show room floor.

Reaching the front of the club, they noticed that there were two different lines. "Ay! King! Yo! King!" Someone was calling his name and waving for him to come to the front of the line.

King was squinting his eyes to see who the guy was that was calling his name and waving him to the front of the line. He finally recognized the guy as Mike-Mike, from Kannapolis.

Twan and King showed the girls to the front of the line with Mike-Mike and his crew. King wanted to deny the request, but was encouraged by Twan to take him up on his offer. They went to the front and waited five minutes to be let inside, since they let King and his crew in line with them, he insisted on paying everyone's entry fee. It was $100 per person since it was New Year's Eve. There were four people in King's group and Mike-Mike had twelve people. Altogether the entry fee came to $1600. Everyone was escorted inside were King paid an additional $2500 for a VIP booth.

King asked Mike-Mike and his crew to join them since they came in together. Mike-Mike wanted to decline but he could use this time as an opportunity to negotiate some prices. After a couple of minutes, Mike-Mike accepted the offer and bottles started popping.

Everyone enjoyed themselves as the liquor flowed. Candy and King danced to almost every song. Twan was dancing, but not as much. He kept his eye on King throughout the night.

There were a lot of people that ran in their circle who were in attendance. So even though they were out of town, they still had to be on point. They partied on special occasions, but it was within their circle.

When the song ended they all returned to the VIP booth to catch their breath. The ladies excused themselves to go to the bathroom and freshen up. King kissed Candy as she walked away.

There was 45 minutes until the New Year would kick in. Mike-Mike came over and sat beside King after coming off the dance floor.

"Are you having a good time?" King asked.

"Yes I am," Mike-Mike replied after pouring himself a shot of 1800. "Business must be slow up your way," King said, sparking up a conversation.

"Naw! It's actually flowing good," Mike-Mike replied. "What would make you think otherwise?" He questioned King.

"You haven't called me in a couple weeks, and it's not like you," King answered.

"Well, to be completely honest with you, I was under the impression that you had gotten a hold of some bad shit," Mike-Mike admitted.

King poured himself a shot as well, hearing this revelation had sparked King's interest. "What would make you assume such a ludicrous idea?" King asked with a smirk on his face.

"I grabbed this joint from this nigga I know down your way," Mike-Mike said, scooting up to get closer to King so that he was guaranteed to hear him. "Basically, it turned out to be all bullshit, then the nigga said it came from you."

"This has got to be the smallest world we live in," King thought to himself. He thought immediately of the fake brick of cocaine that he was robbed of. *"Ain't no fucking way this shit fell in my lap just like this," he considered.* "Whoever you bought the joint from, did they know that we were in business together?" King questioned.

"Of course not!" Mike-Mike exclaimed.

He had to test Mike-Mike to see where his loyalty laid. "Do you feel comfortable telling me who sold you that brick?" King asked, not expecting to get a name exactly, but he crossed fingers, hoping to find out who had come into his house.

"Hell yeah, I'm comfortable my nigga! My loyalty is to you and your father." He stated putting King's mind at ease. "His name is Smoke," Mike-Mike stated.

King could not believe his ears. How would Mike-Mike know to buy a brick from Smoke, that nigga ain't got brick money.

Sensing how King's energy had changed, Mike-Mike asked if he knew Smoke.

King lied and said that he didn't know him personally, but knew of him.

The ladies came back from the bathroom and started taking shots with their men.

Mike-Mike took that has his cue to go mingle with his crew. "I'm gonna go find me a date to take home," Mike-Mike said as he got up to leave. He and King gave each other a pound and agreed to finish the conversation another time.

King sat down confused about what he had just learned. Twan watched him, knowing something had been said and he had missed it.

"This wasn't the time nor the place to be focused on that situation," thought King. He grabbed Candy and started dancing right there in the VIP. Twan and Shonda got on the floor and they all danced for four songs straight.

King looked at his watch and saw that there were only five minutes until the ball dropped. "Yo! Everybody get your cups and fill them up!!" He yelled.

Twan filled Shonda's cup while King filled Candy's. Standing up on the couch, not caring what the bouncers would say, King raise the whole bottle up and said, "I want y'all to know that this has been a wonderful year!!"

"And there is more to come in 2000!!" Twan added as he got on the couch with King.

"10..., 9..., 8..., 7..., 6..., 5..., 4..., 3..., 2..., 1, Happy New Year!!!" Everyone screamed out loud.

After taking their shots and emptying the bottle, another bottle was brought over to the table. They danced the night away as Twan and Shonda got drunk as hell.

It was 12:45 am and King started getting tired. They all agreed that it was time to call it a night. As they were headed out of the club, an altercation had taken place on the side of the club.

Mike-Mike ran up to them with his entourage in tow. "Let's get out of here!" He yelled at King as they made a clearing straight to the exit. Once outside King thanked him as he hurried to the car. King had already popped the trunk as they reached the back of the car.

Once the ladies were in the car, Twan and King pulled their guns out on display and got in the car. While they were leaving the parking lot they could hear gunfire erupt from seemingly every direction.

"Can't go nowhere and have fun," King said as he drove up N. Tyron Street.

They made it back to the motel safely, considering all the alcohol King had drank that night. Since they had a suit, King told Twan they could have the extra guest room instead of leaving, or trying to find a room at this time of night. Twan was cool with it and they chilled.

Candy and Shonda were in the kitchen taking shots. King knew they would be in there for a while. He was out of it. Interrupting his vibe, Twan asked what Mike-Mike was talking about in the club.

King snapped his fingers and sat up. "Man, you wouldn't believe what he said if I told you!"

"Try me," Twan replied, looking serious with his blood shot eyes. He was rolling a blunt while King got his thoughts together.

"He told me that Smoke tried to sell him a brick, but it was all bullshit," King said.

The blunt fell out of Twan's lip as he stared at King. "Say what?" Twan said in disbelief.

King repeated what he said but it still didn't sat right with Twan. He picked up the blunt and fired it up, inhaling deeply. Both men looked at each other, already knowing what the other was thinking.

Chapter 16

Twan and King had been sitting on the porch as traffic slowed. King had started taking hustling more serious since the incident on Christmas Eve. He wanted his presence felt all over Salisbury, not just on the Eastside.

King had started reading books that would strengthen his mind and show him how to strategically plot and plan. 'The Art of War' was the first book he read, then '33 Strategies of War'. And finally, he read 'The 48 Laws of Power'.

As he read those books, King started realizing the potential he had to take over the city. His first plan was to hang a crown on all the powerlines that he saw. The crown was indicating that was his block. *"Kings block."* He did it on Shaver Street, Lee Street, Cemetery Street, Liberty Street, and Fisher Street. He had single-handedly taken over the Eastside. It was accomplished with determination and finesse. Not one bullet had to be shot to establish himself as HNIC.

He manipulated all the hustlers and gave ultimatums. Basically you could only be on the block if you bought cocaine or weed from him or Twan. NO EXCEPTIONS! Nobody could be on the block if they weren't part of NAAM!!

King had taken a liking to a few young and ruthless individuals. Revlon and Skinny were also scheduled to be home by the end of the year. It was the beginning of 2000 and King had to put niggas in place because he was about to start college.

While they were sitting on the porch, Smoke road passed them in a Cadillac DTS on 20's. "You see that black motherfucker?" King asked.

"Yeah! I see his dead ass," Twan replied, staring the man down as he cruised by. "Yo! Have you talked to Mike-Mike?" Twan asked.

"Not since New Year's Eve," King said, thinking of a way to get at Smoke. King's phone rang and he looked at the 919 area code. He knew that it could only be one person calling him. Excited, he jumped off the porch to walk away from Twan to get some privacy.

Twan reached for his gun, thinking someone was trying to bring them a move because of King's sudden movements.

King took a breath and calmed himself so that he could answer the phone. "Hello," he answered nonchalantly and smooth, not wanting to sound eager to talk.

"Yes, this is Emory. Hello?" A feminine voice spoke into his ear.

Hearing her voice made King look at his phone as if someone was playing a prank on him. "Uh…, uh…, yes, this is King," he stammered into the phone.

"My bad King, this is Timiya," she said and started laughing at his uneasiness

"Timiya? Timiya," King kept saying, playing as though he didn't remember her. The phone was completely silent as they sat quietly.

"Timiya from NC State," she blurted out, embarrassed that he hadn't remembered who she was.

"Oh shit! Damn, my bad," King said, finally acknowledging her. "What's going on?" He asked, wanting to see her.

"Nothing much, I was just calling to see if you had any plans for the weekend."

"I don't make plans," he admitted. "I just go with the flow!"

"Sounds good," Timiya responded.

"Are you trying to come down this way?" He asked anxiously.

Timiya pondered his question, not wanting to answer too quickly.

"Maybe I shouldn't have asked her that," he thought.

"He wants to see me," she thought to herself, blushing. "I might be able to come if you were interested in seeing me. But I don't want to cause any problems between you and Candy," she lied.

King knew that she and Candy had been conversing often. "First, I know that you know I have a girl," King emphasized. "Secondly, it's up to you if you wanna come, long as we have that understood." King loved Candy, but he wanted to see what this chick was working with.

"Ok. Well, I'll call you later this week if I do decide to come," Timiya stated.

"Ok," King replied, wanting her to be the one to make that decision.

"Nice talking to you again," she said and hung up the phone.

After hanging up, King grabbed his dick, anticipating sliding it between those thick red thighs.

Twan sat on the porch laughing as he watched King prance around the front yard like George Jefferson. It was a sight to see. "Who was that player?" Twan asked.

King's smile was beaming from ear to ear. "That, my boy, was Timiya, the tour guide from NC State. It's a thick red bone, with long hair, that looks Brazilian and she's real ass phat like Ronnie from players club."

Twan laughed at his friend as he described Timiya. Then, as they were talking, a sale pulled up. "What's good J-Bo?" Twan asked.

"Ain't shit man. Let me get a ball and a ball," he stated after handing Twan $300.

That would get him 3.5 g of crack and 3.5 g of powder. Twan got up to go grab the product for him and saw that Smoke was riding through again.

J-Bo saw how King was watching him ride by with venom in his eyes. If looks could kill, Smoke would surely be dead. "You got a problem with that nigga?" J-Bo asked.

"Naw. Why you say that?" King probed, not wanting to let on that he did.

"I can feel the tension and your whole demeanor changed," he said. "I also asked because I know where he be laying his head," J-Bo admitted.

King didn't trust many people. He knew J-Bo, but not enough to trust him with certain information. "I'll keep that in mind for real," King said as Twan came out of the house.

"Let me know," J-Bo said after grabbing his product. He winked at King as he walked off to get back in his car.

"Let you know what?" Twan asked, wanting to know what had been said while he was inside.

"While you were inside Smoke came back through. J-Bo caught me eyeballing him and asked if we had beef? I said no off the muscle. He must have sensed I was lying, because he said he knew where Smoke laid his head."

Twan's eyebrows went up.

"Shocked the hell out of me too," King said.

"Can we trust this nigga?" Twan question skeptically.

"Only time will tell," King answered. "He definitely gonna take us to this nigga."

Days went by as King stayed away from the block. It was Friday and Timiya still hadn't reached out to King. Playoffs were about to begin and King would announce publicly what college he would be attending soon. His relationship with Candy had been good since New Year's Eve, but lately she had been a recluse. She seldomly wanted to hang out with King in public and she refused to go anywhere alone.

King had to kill Smoke and his accomplice. Coming to this realization prompted him to call Twan.

"Yo!" Twan answered on the first ring.

"Do you still have the dude J-Bo's number?" King asked.

"Yeah, I got it," Twan answered, already knowing where the conversation was going. "I'll put it in motion as soon as we get off the phone," Twan replied, then he hung up.

"I'm tired of letting shit slide. His ass is grass tonight!" King thought. Thinking about Candy put him in an uncomfortable situation. She was scared to come outside and she should never have to feel like that, or live like that.

When King walked into the bedroom, Candy was lying across the bed, flipping through channels. "Whatcha watching?" King asked just to start a conversation. It was almost 6 PM and they were cooped up in the house.

"Channel surfing," she responded with annoyance in her voice.

"Well, I found out who one of the guys were that ran in our house and I'm going to take care of it," King said, assuring Candy.

She slowly set up in bed. "Baby, please don't get into any trouble," Candy begged with concern written all over her face. "Can you let Twan or somebody else handle the situation?" She asked, almost pleading.

"I could, but it happened to me! To us!" King said as he got up off the bed, clenching his fists. "I can't allow someone to come up in our house, threaten us and take something from us."

"That shit didn't mean nothing!" She yelled at him.

"I gotta make an example out of this nigga! Show these motherfuckers that I am not to be fucked with!" King yelled and stormed out of the room.

She put her head down, defeated. She already knew that his mind was made up. She got up off the bed and went downstairs to see where King had gone off to. She found him outside on the patio, in the backyard.

He was rolling a blunt when he gazed up and saw Candy approaching him. He sat the blunt down and pulled a chair out for her to sit beside him. He picked up the blunt, then fired it up and they sat in silence while he took a few pulls from it.

Candy was the first to speak. "Listen, I understand exactly what you're saying and where you're coming from. But I need you to understand that you have a lot to lose. I don't want you throwing your life away for nothing."

As King smoked, he looked directly at Candy. "How can you say I would be throwing my life away for nothing? You are my everything!" He explained. "When them niggas came into the house that night, they took a piece of you with them," King exclaimed. "You haven't been yourself ever since. You don't go out as much anymore and you don't allow me to take you anywhere. It's like you're scared to be around me unless we're in the house," King confessed. "I will not live like this or have you living like this." He stopped to take a pull off the blunt he was smoking and he noticed tears roll down Candy's face like diamond droplets.

Candy sobbed uncontrollably as she wiped the tears from her face. "I've been like this the past couple of weeks because," Candy paused for a minute as she contemplated what she wanted to say.

"Because what?" King asked, agitated.

"Because I'm pregnant!" She shouted. She stared at King to see if she could decipher his reaction to her confession.

Surprisingly, he stood up and grabbed her hands so that he could see her stomach. He picked her up and spun her around excitedly. He then put her down quickly, thinking that he was hurting her and the baby.

"Hell yeah!" He yelled, fist pumping. "How many months are you?" King questioned her.

"I'm not sure, I have to make a doctor's appointment," she replied.

This blessing gave him even more determination to handle the situation with Smoke immediately. And as the thought crossed his mind, his phone rang. It was Twan.

"Yeah," King answered, hyped to go put in some work. "Ok I'm on my way," he said and hung up the phone.

As he got up, he kissed Candy on the lips and said, "That was Twan. Something important just came up, I have to go."

As he sprinted to his car, Candy called out, "Be careful!" Then she realized that she had no idea what the rush was all about.

King desperately wanted to get this over with now that he had a child on the way. He had to guarantee his and Candy's safety at all costs. When he got into his car, he put in Pastor Troy's new song, "Vice Versa." He blasted the song repeatedly as he sped through traffic, making it to the Eastside and record breaking time.

When he pulled up J-Bo was out back with Twan, they were both blacked out from head to toe. Seeing them made King realize that he wasn't dressed for the occasion.

"Fuck it," he said and got ready to handle his business.

"What's the business?" J-Bo said giving him a pound.

"Let's get to it," King stated.

They went inside Smooth's house on Fisher Street. Smooth was the house man and the house was full of fiends getting high in all the back rooms.

"What's the plan?" Twan asked J-Bo.

"Smoke is always sitting on the porch on Knox Street. Whenever he make a play, he goes across the street to the store," J-Bo explained. "I'ma call him and say I want a half time and when he comes to the store, y'all got'em," J-Bo said nonchalantly.

"That shit sounds too easy," King said.

"I'm certain of the play. He thinks he's untouchable because them blood niggas be out there with him," J-Bo explained. "He won't expect nothing. That's my word."

"Aye, Smooth. Let me holler at you right quick," King said, escorting him to the back room.

When King walked out of the room, Twan asked J-Bo, "Are you sure that's gonna be that easy?" Twan was looking at him in the eyes with the coldest black eyes J-Bo had ever seen.

"I'm positive," J-Bo answered seriously.

At that moment King came back with a set of car keys in his hand. "Make the call," he said, jingling the keys in their faces. "We're taking the van parked outside."

They left and jumped in the van to head to some apartments that were parked beside the store. J-Bo would call them when he was on the way to the store. From where they parked, they had a clear view of the store's parking lot and entrance, all they had to do is wait.

Fifteen minutes had passed as they sat and waited for the call. Twan was getting impatient and wanted to call J-Bo when his phone rang. It was J-Bo, indicating that it was show time.

King cranked the van up and waited to see J-Bo pull up. A couple minutes later a brown Chevy pulled up with 20s. It was J-Bo, he sat in his car patiently, waiting for Smoke to come from across the street.

It took about five minutes, but lo and behold, Smoke came bopping across the street as though he didn't have a care in the world. He wasn't by himself as they had thought though, there was another guy with him who had a red do rag hanging out of his right pocket.

"Fuck it!" Twan said. "He got to get it too! "

They sat in the van, waiting patiently as Smoke got situated in J-Bo's car. Once they saw the door close, King eased the van out of the apartments and crept up to the store's parking lot.

"You're ready?" Twan asked while sliding his mask on.

"Hell yeah!" King said with venom in his voice.

King pulled directly behind J-Bo's car and Twan jumped out with a gun on the blood nigga. King hurried out of the van and ran to the passenger side of J-Bo's car.

Smoke sat there looking around, dumbfounded as to what was taking place right in front of him. It all happened so fast, Twan was walking the other nigga at gunpoint to the van and King had pulled Smoke out of the car as well. J-Bo jumped out his car, then jumped into the driver side of the van.

Once everyone was back in the van, J-Bo eased out of the parking lot, nice and smooth. They drove for about ten minutes in silence before they pulled up to an abandoned building on E. Horah Street. The building was beside the railroad tracks and the laundromat was around the corner. Nobody would hear or see anything. J-Bo pulled the van behind the building with the lights out.

"Get your bitch ass out of the van!" King demanded, smacking Smoke upside the head with the gun.

Both men had taken their masks off, they knew he would not survive the ordeal. When Smoke's eyes adjusted in the darkness of the building, he damn near shit on himself when he saw that Twan and King were behind his kidnapping.

King walked up to Smoke and said, "Like you told me when you ran up in my house! You know what we're here for!" He smack the hell out of Smoke, who had fallen on the ground. "Now, I'm going to ask you one time and one time only," he said, standing over top of Smoke. "Who was with you that night at my house?"

Silence fell through the building. "Stand his ass up!" King demanded.

J-Bo went and yanked Smoke up roughly by his collar.

"Empty their pockets," King said while pacing back-and-forth, scratching his head with the 40 Cal in his hand.

Twan handed all their belongings over to King, who threw them on the ground. "You have thirty seconds to answer me, or my partner is going to kill your homie."

Smoke looked at his homie, then back at King.

"Ten seconds," King whispered with a sinister grin on his face.

Before the ten seconds ran out, Smoke's homey yelled, "It was Cash! It was Cash!"

"How was that so hard?" King asked as he walked up to the guy and pouted at his head like a dog. He turned around and walked away from the guy.

"Twan!" King called his name.

"Boom! Boom! Boom!" Twan had walked up to the guy and shot him three times, point blank in the face. J-Bo jumped when Twan shot the dude.

King, still in front of Smoke who had his hands crossed in front of his pelvic area, asked, "Do you have anything you want to say to me before I kill you?"

"Damn! Do you smell that?" Twan asked, scrunching up his face.

"What the fuck?" King yelled. "It smells like shit. Turn your ass around," King said to Smoke pointing the gun at him.

Smoke stood defiantly, looking King straight in his eyes, refusing to turn around.

King walked up behind him, standing close to his ear. He whispered into his ear, "You fucked with the wrong nigga!" Then he stepped back and smoked the shit out of him with his gun.

Smoke fell to the ground with a hard thud, holding the back of his head, but that was the least of his worries. Twan kicked him in the face, which made him end up on his back. Once he looked up, his expression was like a deer caught in the headlights. King unloaded the whole clip into Smoke's body. Twan did the same thing.

King was still squeezing the trigger, not realizing that he had run out of bullets. He was in a zone. His chest was racing up and down at a rapid pace and he had spit in the corners of his mouth.

"You ok?" Twan asked, walking up to his friend. Twan took his gun as he looked down at the gruesome corpse. King was reluctant to let the gun go.

After taking the gun, Twan looked at J-Bo, who stood frozen in his spot. Both King and Twan looked at each other and then back to J-Bo who was still standing there like a mannequin. The man was in total shock.

They walk towards the van and King asked Twan if he could get his gun back. Twan was hesitant at first, but when he obliged, King took the gun and turned around, facing smoke's lifeless body. He paused for about five seconds, as if he was going to continue to shoot the already dead man. Then he raise the gun and pointed it directly in J-Bo's face.

"Whoa! What the fuck's going on man? Twan! Get ya man. Twan! I ain't gonna say shit!" J-Bo stuttered, backpedaling.

King fired multiple rounds into J-Bo's face and chest without a word.

Twan was shocked at what had just happened. "What was that about?" He questioned King.

"You asked me if I smelled that shit. I smelled it, but it wasn't smoke! Therefore, it had to be J-Bo. I had to kill him for one reason alone," King explained. "He couldn't hold his own shit. So I knew that I couldn't trust him to hold ours," King stated flatly. "Get the keys out the van and burn that bitch."

Twan did as he was told while King walked to the entrance of the building. King thought about how they would get Cash as the van erupted into flames. King felt the heat from the van, but wondered what was taking Twan so long. He turned around and noticed he was throwing a body into the burning van. Twan walked up to him sweating like a slave. King was smoking a fresh blunt that he had pulled out of his pocket.

"Let me hit that shit," Twan demanded.

King handed Twan the blunt and they both walked away from the burning building into the night.

Chapter 17

Cash was floating around the city at snail's pace on March 9th, 2000. Smoke had somehow gotten himself killed, which put Cash on high alert. When he and Smoke pistol whipped King's, uncle, and then force their way into King's house, he never thought about the repercussions. Somehow they figured out that it was Smoke. That made him question whether or not Smoke had given him up before he was killed. All Cash could do was stay strapped and continue to get money.

King had a crew that would kill and die for him. While Cash rode around the city, he noticed that crowns had been hung from powerlines on almost every block that he passed. King had claimed his turf! He had been doing his thang on the streets and on the basketball court.

Salisbury High School was playing in the semifinals conference game this week. If they won, that would put them in the State Championship game, which was going to be played at Wake Forest University. Everyone knew that King was going to go pro. He would more than likely play one year at NC State and be done.

DC had quit hustling and was reaping the rewards while enjoying life. Nobody or nothing could stop him, or so he thought.

The game was a week away and it was Tuesday. Everybody worldwide knew that Tuesday's and Thursday's were the hottest days for a hustler. Kareem and DC had been on their way to one of several beauty salons on the Westside when Kareem noticed that a black on black Illuminar had been following them as they turned the last corners.

"Hey, I think we're being followed," he whispered, nudging DC.

DC was worried because he knew that they knew he was clean. Also, he hadn't had any dealings with drugs in the past two years. "We good," he informed his friend as he looked in the car's side mirror. "The only way to know for sure if you're being followed, is to make four right turns. Circle the block," DC demanded to see if his assumption was indeed correct.

Doing as he was told, Karim turned the next corner taking a right, and so did the Illuminar. They approach the next corner and made another right. Once again, so did the Illuminar.

"Something ain't right," Kareem said as they got ready to make the third turn.

When they were about to turn, DC had had enough and yelled for Kareem to pull over. "Pull this bitch over! I'm gonna see what the fuck they want!" He demanded.

Kareem slowly pulled over and DC was out of the car before it had even stopped. Kareem put the car in park and got out along with his boss. Suddenly they were swarmed by ATF, DEA, and FBI agents. They were jumping out of multiple cars, coming from all directions.

The agent in the black on black Illuminar that had been following them told DC, "Put your hands behind your back. You have the right to remain silent. Anything you say, can and will be used against you in the court of law," the agent stated, reading him his Miranda rights.

DC did as he was told while his mind tried to register where this heat could be coming from. Kareem had been handcuffed as well. Both men were escorted to the Salisbury Police Department for further questioning and interrogation.

An hour later, both men had been charged with possession of a firearm by a convicted felon, distribution of cocaine and money laundering. On his indictment, it stated that DC had sold ten bricks in 1996 to a man in Statesville, NC. Three days following that it was stated that seven bricks had been sold in Charlotte, NC.

King sat outside of the Rowan County Detention Center for hours, waiting on his father to call him. King had been riding through the city when he spotted his father's car. He instantly turned a few corners to try to catch up with him, but when he finally did, DC had been swarmed by agents of all sorts.

King had sat back at a very discreet distance and watch things unfold. Fortunately, it wasn't about no murder, because of all the letters displayed across the front and back of the agent's jackets.

King sat and thought carefully about what his dad would do. Automatically he dialed their lawyer's number, who answered on the first ring.

"Yes, this is Mr. Ginn. I've been waiting for you to call for hours," he stated.

"What's going on with my father?" King asked anxiously.

"Your father has stepped into some shit. I'm trying to get all the specifics as we speak," Mr. Ginn replied. "I have instructions for you to stay away from all the businesses and off of the streets. You are to go to school and focus on your basketball career," Mr. Ginn informed him.

He listened to his advisor, not knowing how this was going to play out. "Can you tell my father I said to call me?" King asked.

"I'm hoping to have him out in the next week, when he goes to court for his pretrial release hearing," Mr. Ginn said.

"Do you think he will be released?" King questioned hesitantly.

"Yes. Based on your father not being a repeat offender, or having a criminal history. I don't think anything will hinder him from being released," Mr. Ginn insisted. "I'm going to need you, or anybody that's legit, to come to his arraignment when I notify you," Mr. Ginn stated.

"Sure," King assured him. "Tell my father I love him and to keep his head up," King said and then hung up the phone and just sat there, motionless, not knowing what to do.

He pulled off and drove the thirty minute drive to his house, where Candy was waiting for him. She felt terrible that DC had gotten locked up. For the time being, King was left to fend for her and himself. Even though he had been taking care of himself for a while, DC was all the family he had except for his uncle and his homies.

When King got out of the car, Candy walked into his arms and just held onto him and rubbed his back soothingly. She wanted him to know she was there for him and would be by his side through the whole ordeal.

"Come on, let's go inside," Candy said, grabbing him by the hand and leading him into the house.

The following week went by in slow motion. King had been going to school as usual. He was questioned about his father by teachers and coaches too. They all wanted to make sure his mind was stable so that nothing would interfere with his college plans.

It was Friday the 16th and Lynn, Candy, Lauren, and King were all outside the federal courthouse in Greensboro. It was 9 am and the group was scheduled to meet the lawyer at 9:30 am. As they were waiting on the lawyer, King's anxiety was at an all-time high. He was trying his best to contain it. In all the years that his father hustled, he had never been caught with anything.

Now that he hadn't touched any drugs in the past couple of years, he was trapped. It was hard for King to fathom.

Interrupting his thoughts, Mr. Ginn walked briskly upon the group and introduced himself. They all headed to the courthouse and into the court room where they were told to be seated. Mr. Ginn left to have a conversation with DC, who was being transferred from the jail to the courthouse.

As they waited, other lawyers were arriving and talking with some of their client's family members. There was a small crowd that morning, maybe ten people at the most. 9:30 had approached without anyone noticing it and Mr. Ginn came out from the back, taking a seat in the first row with the other attorneys.

The judge walked in and everybody stood simultaneously. The bailiff spoke then everyone took their seats. Two cases were heard before it was DC's turn to be brought into the quart room. As he was escorted to the table where his lawyer sat, he kept his head held high. There were no bags under his eyes, so you could tell that he slept comfortably, with no worries.

When he glanced at the crowd, he noticed his family. He smiled, then winked at them, as if everything was good and he wasn't sitting in a federal court room.

DC sat down so that he and his lawyer could converse. Then the district attorney stood and recited DC's government name, his docket number and his charges. After reading his charges, he continued to state how much each charge carried. Each charge carried 0 to 20 years and he had three counts.

After the charges had been discussed, the judge asked to hear the motions about bond. Mr. Ginn stood up and started telling the judge how DC was a pillar of the community. Also, how he had given past felons jobs in some of his establishments. He also mentioned that DC didn't have any significant charges in the past 20 years that would make him a flight risk and that he has a son that was present and was raising by himself.

Ginn turned around and asked King to stand. When he stood, Mr. Ginn continued and talked about how King was in his senior year of high school and how he had scholarships from almost 20 division 1's.

King sat down after Mr. Ginn started speaking of other matters.

"As you can see your honor, these allegations stem from 1996. Whoever the individual is making these harsh assumptions, they have to been incarcerated. They are trying to shift the attention from their own situation to my client. I am asking that my client, Mr. Cummings, be released to serve house arrest until he is prosecuted. I think anyone would say that is reasonable. Thank you your honor," Ginn said and sat down.

The district attorney stood and gave his spiel about DC being a dangerous man. That all his establishments were acquired by drug money. How ex-felons that he employs are probably part of his drug organization.

"Objection!" Mr. Ginn stated. "That comment has nothing to do with my client being here today."

"Sustained!" The judge yelled.

"There's nothing more I have to say or honor," the district attorney replied, sitting down visibly upset.

"Will the defense please stand at this moment," the judge insisted.

DC and his lawyer stood at the same time.

"Mr. Carter, you have been charged with some serious allegations that carry a lot of time. I've looked at your criminal history, which shows that you have kept your nose clean." The judge looked at DC with admiration and continued. "I must say that you being a single father and raising your son, makes you seem to really be a standup guy. Giving you that comment is something I rarely do because you're still standing in my court room," The judge stated. "How old are you Mr. Cummings?" The judge asked.

"I'm 52 years old, your honor," DC answered.

"It's the year 2000 and your son is about to graduate high school. He's going to need you to guide and assist him through life. Therefore, based on your criminal history and not being a flight risk, I'm going to set your bond at $100,000. I wish you the best. You will be on an ankle monitor until the day you are released. Next case," the judge said while slamming down her gavel.

Chapter 18

Two months passed and things were turning from bad to worse. King had helped Salisbury high school win the state championship and he announced that he was going to attend NC State the following year.

He got news from his father that all of their businesses were being closed. All the accounts were being frozen too. DC had to be in court September 9th. He also recently found out that he had cancer. They had been going through a terrible time. They say when it rains, it pours and it was starting to pour.

King had made arrangements for Candy's mom, Lauren, and Len to be married at DC's mini mansion. That way DC would be able to attend the special occasion. There was well over 300 people in attendance. DC had Charlie Wilson come to sing. The venue was like something you would only see in a celebrity wedding magazine. Someone would have thought there was a celebrity getting married, instead of a smoker, turned hustler who got out of the game.

King watched from a distance, he was happy and sad at the same time. He was happy because his uncle kept his word to Lauren and got out of the game. He was sad because of the thought of losing his father to prison and eventually to cancer if he didn't beat it.

Everything he was achieving in life, there would be no one to share it with. He knew that Candy would always be there, but the most important people who matter the most, would not be there to share it with him. His mother and his father.

King must have had pity written all over his face. His father came over in a somber manner and he couldn't look his father in the face because he had tears in his eyes. He refused to show weakness in front of his father, he kept his face down so his father wouldn't notice.

DC knew this was hard for King to swallow, but he had to man up! From the beginning, he told King and showed him that this was a man's world and in this game you will win some and you will lose some. It's never about if things like this would happen, but more about 'when' it will happen.

"King! Listen to me and listen well."

King looked up into his father's face with teary eyes.

"We both knew this day would come and we welcomed it. So now that it is here, we have to take the next step that comes with it," DC explained. "I have to do my time and fight this cancer. There is no way around the situation that I have been faced with. I want you to continue to be the best damn hustler ever come through here. But, before that, I want you to be the best nigga ever come from here on that basketball court."

King smiled as his father gave him motivation and jewels.

"Even if you decide to quit hustling, I am cool with your decision," DC stated.

"I am never gonna stop hustling Dad, because it's in my blood," King confessed. "I got things lined up and I'm certain you will be proud of me when it's all over."

"I am proud of you already," DC said. "And now let's go over here and enjoy your uncle's night. I wish Chuckie was here to see this," DC said, missing his brother.

"Me too," King chimed in. "He would've been proud of his brother."

Twan and Shonda had just came in and was talking to everybody. Everyone was walking around, waiting for the wedding to start, which would be in thirty minutes. Photographers were taking pictures as couples were being seated and greeted by other people.

Charlie Wilson was crooning to one of his old tunes as the crowd sang along with him. It was beautiful.

Candy came over and kissed King on his lips. "Hello sexy!" She said feeling sexy in her Louis Vuitton maternity dress.

"Hey beautiful," he replied.

"I want to thank you and your father for doing this."

"It's nothing baby. We are all family now," he replied.

"I hope our wedding is as beautiful as this," Candy expressed her feelings, looking around at all the lavish decorations.

"It will be more extravagant than this, I assure you," he insisted.

Candy could tell something was bothering him. "What's on your mind bae?" She questioned.

"Oh nothing," he lied. "I'm just caught in the moment."

Chapter 19

King had been really stressed out lately. He was focused on school, but his mind wandered at times. Thinking about his future, he knew some things were about to change. Candy was pregnant with his first child, his father was on his way to prison while fighting cancer, and he was on his way to college. Also, Skinny and Revlon would be home in 90 days.

Candi walked up behind him, interrupting his thoughts. "Mmmm, you smell good," she said inhaling the cool water cologne he had on.

King turned around wrapping his arms around her. "Good morning my love," he said, placing soft kisses on her lips. "Have you spoken to your mom since she returned from her honeymoon?" He asked.

She shook her head no, while sinking into him. She enjoyed being in his arms as usual. "Bae, I'm about to go shopping for some clothes for the baby and a few other things. I should be back in an hour, do you need me to pick you up anything while I'm out?" She asked.

"Yeah. Grab me a pair of all-white Air Force 1's and a sweat suit," King answered.

She kissed him then walked away. He noticed how flat her ass had gotten as he grabbed himself. Seeing the way her ass jiggled made him want a quickie right now. He decided against it because they wouldn't have gotten anything done that day.

He fired a blunt up and got ready to start his day. He showered and got dressed, then was out the door to chase that money. As he turned a few corners his phone rang. Oh! Shit! It was Timiya calling. *"Probably trying to dick tease me again,"* he thought. He wasn't excited about talking to her because she stood him up last time. Going against his better judgement he answered the phone anyway.

"Hello." He answered dryly.

"Is this a bad time to be calling?" She asked, sensing the irritation in his voice.

"Not really. What's up?"

"Well, I'm in Salisbury and I wanted to come see you for a few if you got time," she told him.

Not wanting to sound too eager, he sat silent on the phone for a few seconds. As if they were reading each other's mind, they both asked, "Do you got blunts?" Then started laughing.

"I got the weed," he said.

"I'll get the blunts," she said. "I'm staying at Comfort Suites," Timiya said. After giving him the room number, she hung up.

"I gotta beat that pussy up," King said looking at himself in the rearview mirror.

While on his way to the room he stopped at the BP gas station to grab some condoms and more blunts. When he came out of the store he saw Cash riding down the street with one of his homies in the passenger seat.

"I'm going to kill that nigga," he mumbled to himself.

Cash had been hiding out real good lately. King hadn't had a chance to get the drop on him, but his time was coming.

King got in his car and was pulling up to the motel ten minutes later. He sat in the car, contemplating whether or not he should fuck her. Thinking with his little head made it an easy decision to make.

Riding up the elevator to the fourth floor, then standing in front of room 1213, he hesitated to knock. Realizing it was too late to turn around, he knocked on the door twice. As he anticipated what was about to take place, his dick became hard as a brick.

Nobody asked who it was but the door finally opened. Standing there in a Victoria Secret see through lace pant and bra set, was the thickest red bone he had ever laid eyes on. You could see her pussy lips through her panties and her nipples were hard as hell.

"Damn! Are you gonna come in or just stand there?" She asked with a smirk on her face.

Walking into the room, King could smell the jasmine scented perfume in the air because it was the same kind that Candy wore. King sat on the couch admiring Timiya's beauty and physique.

"So, how are you?" He asked, making small talk.

"I'm good, can't complain," she replied.

"What brings you to Salisbury?"

"Well, to be honest, I felt bad because I never got a chance to reach back out to you since last time. Also, me and Candy have plans for tonight," she boldly stated.

He stood up instantly, expecting Candy to walk through the door at any minute. "What the fuck you on?" King shouted.

"Calm down nigga!" Timiya yelled. "Ain't nobody tryin to set you up or none of the bullshit you thinking. I want some dick, that's it! Nothing more," she said aggressively. She approached him, walking seductively.

King had that look in his eye, like ain't no way he was turning down that pussy! "You trying to fuck me now, then go out and party with my girl later?" He asked, not believing his predicament. "What type of shit are you on?"

"Look! It's like this," she stated, getting frustrated. "Candy and I are cool. It just so happens I wanted to fuck you from the beginning. She and I became cool over time, but my attraction to you remained. Evidently you want something too, because you're here."

Considering she was all the way right, King instantly started busting a blunt. He threw her the blunts, pulled out his weed and the condoms, then told her to roll her own blunt.

Walking through the mall carefree, Candy stopped at almost every store. She had so many bags that she had to get a buggy to carry all of them. She walked into Finish line and noticed Cash and one of his homies. She immediately turned around and walked out of the store, she was aware of the beef that was brewing between him and King. She walked to the closest exit while pulling the buggy of bags, which were slowing her down. Trying to put distance between her and Cash, she forgotten to get King's shoes and outfit.

"Damn!" She said out loud. She headed back in and this time decided to hit Athlete's Foot and Styles. After grabbing the things for King, she found herself getting hungry. She went to the food court and ordered some Chinese food.

When she had finished eating, she went to the car and began to put the bags in the trunk.

"Candy is that you?" A male's voice asked.

Startled, she turned around to see DC. Upon seeing him, she exhaled a deep breath that had gotten caught in her throat.

DC noticed the change in her demeanor and asked, "Is everything all right?"

Unconsciously, she put her hand to her chest to slow down her breathing. "Yes! I'm fine, you just caught me off guard," she lied.

"Where is my son?" He asked, wondering why he would let her be out here alone while pregnant.

"He was at the house when I left not too long ago," she replied.

"OK, well I'll see y'all later. I have to go home and change this ankle monitor," DC stated, then pulled off.

"What has gotten into me?" She asked herself. Seeing Cash put paranoia in her heart. Getting inside the car and get back home was all she wanted to do. She was starting to get nauseous all of the sudden.

"Damn, you're sexy as hell," King said while passing the blunt back to Timiya.

"I hear that all the time" she replied arrogantly. "But thank you!"

As King started feeling the effects of the Hydro, he became hornier. Timiya finish the last of the blunt and put the roach in the ashtray. She stood up and grabbed him, leading him towards the bed.

"Take all your clothes off," she demanded.

"I see you like to take charge," King said smiling.

"No, not really, I just know what it is I want," she commented.

After removing his clothes and standing their butt naked she told him to lie down on the bed. He obliged and stretched out on the bed. She walked to the table and grabbed her phone, going through her playlist she started playing, Trick Daddy's song 'Tonight' featuring Jaheim. This turned King on because now he knew she was a freak.

When she turned around King had stroked his dick to full attention. Seeing how excited he was, Timiya started dancing provocatively. She unstrapped her bra to release some of the prettiest, perky breasts known to man.

"Damn, I'm about to fuck the shit out of this bitch," King thought to himself.

She slid her panties off slowly while bending over with her ass facing King. Her middle finger was going in and out of her tunnel slowly, he could see all the cum on her finger every time it exited. The pussy was salivating. She crawled from the foot of the bed up in between his legs. Without any indication, she took a hold of his manhood and devoured it hungrily. She deep throated it without gagging or choking. Her head bobbing up and down at different places, fast, then, slow, with spit all over his stick.

She would spit on the dick, then slurp up all the juices in one motion. He was being tortured, he couldn't take it anymore. He grabbed her by her hair and started fucking her mouth viciously.

"Oh! Shit bitch! Damn, I can't hold it! Argh!" He exploded a full load in her mouth while humping faster. Timiya was taking that shit like a pro, choking momentarily but it didn't stop her head from bobbing.

"Ah! God damn Timiya," he said out of breath.

She kept on sucking while he ran his hands through her hair. Feeling as if he was gonna come again, he started talking more shit. "Don't stop! Don't stop bitch! Pull that nut up out of this dick. Oh! Oh! Damn, I'm bout to bust again!"

Hearing this turned Timiya on. She started massaging his nut sack softly. She was so turned on by him yelling that she climaxed as well. She had been playing with her clit the whole time she was sucking him off. Once she thought she had sucked him dry, she sucked for a few more seconds to make sure. Making sure that she had gotten him back erect, she said, "Let me ride this motherfucker," as she mounted him looking dead in his eyes. When she squatted down, she said, "Oh shit," not realizing that her pussy was tighter than she remembered.

"That pussy tight as fuck," King stated, watching her sit down on his pole. When she got her rhythm going good, King started pounding into her every time she came down.

"Ouch! Ouch! Slow down baby," Timiya demanded, placing her hands on his chest to avoid the deadly strokes he was slamming into her.

King rammed in and out fast as he could, grabbing her by the shoulders forcefully. Timiya couldn't take it, but he continued thrusting as if his life depended on him digging in.

Candy was almost home when she noticed a car behind her playing loud music. Looking in the rearview mirror, she about shit when she saw it was Cash. Nervously, she picked up her phone to call King. The phone rang several times before going to voicemail.

"Damn!" She shouted, hitting the steering wheel. Now she was really nervous. She tried calling again. This time it rang numerous times. Not knowing who else to call, she dialed her mom's number.

Lauren answered on the first ring. "Hello!"

"Mom, there's a guy following me that King's been having problems with," she said frantically into the phone.

"Where are you?" Her mom asked concerned.

"I'm coming down Highway 29."

Boom! Boom! Boom!

"Oh! Shit! What the hell was that?" Lauren asked, scared for her daughter's life.

"Mama! He's shooting at me! Oh my Goooooood!" Candy cried hysterically into the phone as she drove recklessly, trying to dodge the bullet and drive. "Ma! They trying to pull up beside me. I'm trying to speed up but I can't lose them," she cried.

Boom! Boom! Argg! Aarrggg! Crash! Whomp!!

"Hello! Hello! Candy say something baby, please!" Lauren begged. "Oh my God!" Lauren kept calling Candy's name, but got no answer. She didn't know what to do except have the police ride up Highway 29. Hopefully they find her in time to give her some assistance.

King heard his phone ringing nonstop back to back, but the pussy was so good. He refused to stop. He was in a trance. Timiya was riding his dick like her life depended on it.

"Get up and turnover," King instructed her.

She got up off the dick, sweating profusely. When she laid back King was on top, mounting her instantly. He was back in her love tunnel pounding away.

"What the fuck you doing to me?" She yelled as she grabbed the sheets.

King threw one of her legs onto his shoulder. This made him pound harder and faster into her.

"Oh, baby! Beat this pussy up." She began grabbing his ass cheeks.

Timiya was making the sexiest fuck faces he had ever seen. "This is the best pussy I ever had," he said, then gritted his teeth.

"Mmm! Mmm! I want this dick in me every day," she said. "Please! Please fuck me every day!!"

Hearing her talk like that was driving King wild. "I'm about to nut again! Oh! Shit! I want you to swallow that shit," King demanded. "Get ready bitch! Damn, come here!! Ooh! Come here," he said with urgency.

He pulled out of her and Timiya jumped up like the bed was on fire. She took King in her mouth just as he exploded.

"What the fuuuuck!!" King said, humping her face while on his knees. He rubbed his fingers through her hair lovingly.

She stopped and swallowed as if he was putting life back into her body, while she suck the life out of him.

"Damn suck that shit baby." King was exhausted. "Swallow all that shit," he demanded, out of breath.

Timiya stroked and sucked him until his dick went limp. His dick fell out of her mouth like a gummy worm.

Kings phone was ringing nonstop as he laid back, panting heavily. He couldn't move if he wanted to. After catching his breath, he finally made it to the phone. He saw that they were missed calls from Candy, Lauren, DC, and Twan.

Seeing all the missed calls prompted him to check his messages and voicemails. When he opened his first message, he drop the phone and hurried to put his clothes on. He wanted to pass out, but his adrenaline was running so high. He grabbed his stuff and was out the door so fast that he accidentally left his phone.

Timiya picked up the phone and saw a message stating that Candy had been shot and was taken to the hospital.

Chapter 20

December 20th 2000. Sitting in the hospital for the past three days had been the longest days of King's life. Now that he was home, all he wanted to do was hear Candy's voice.

Candy had been shot multiple times. She suffered gunshot wounds to her ribs and one to the chest. After being shot, she ran the car off the road and into a street pole. She was barely conscious when the ambulance arrived.

Upon arriving at the hospital, they performed multiple surgeries on her, trying to save the baby, but to no avail. The baby was lost and Candy had slipped into a coma. They tried everything they could, with some of the best surgeons. But, on the third day of her being comatose, she went into convulsions. There was nothing else that could be done to save her.

Lynn was assisting Lauren with making the funeral arrangements.

"Yo! King!" Twan was trying to pass him the blunt.

King was in his own world. "I can't believe this shit," he said taking the blunt. "If I wasn't fucking with that bitch Timiya, I would have answered my damn phone," King stated, upset and constantly blaming himself for what happened to Candy.

Twan questioned the thoughts going through his best friends mind. King smoked while fighting his demons that were sure to take him down if he didn't get himself together.

"FUCK THIS SHIT!" Twan said, pounding the table. "LET'S GO!" He demanded, standing up. "We bout to go find this nigga right now! It's already been three days with $100,000 on this motherfuckers head, I'm positive somebody heard or knows where this cocksucker is."

Feeling the same way, King instructed Twan to make some calls to see about the feelers they had put out. "I'm gonna jump in the shower so I can get my head together," King said getting up. "Be ready when I get myself together!"

"That's what the fuck I'm talking about," Twan stated getting hyped, knowing they were about to hit the streets.

Cash had been cruising the streets of Salisbury without a care in the world. After what took place a couple of days ago, he had assumed he was now the HNIC of Salisbury. He had bragged about killing King and he had told his soldiers in Conrad how he followed King from the mall in his black DTS Cadillac. They were coming down Highway 29 when Cash blazed up the Caddy, hitting him multiple times. He told how afterwards they watched the car veer off the road and into a street pole. That was three days ago and now Cash was feeling like he was on top of the world.

His phone started ringing and Cash turned down the music in his car so that he could answer it. He smiled seeing this freak bitch named Kiki on his screen. He automatically thought she wanted some powder.

"Yeah!" He said, not wanting to sound eager.

Kiki started asking questions, but as the conversation continued Cash had to pull over. "Are you sure about what you're saying?" He asked, vexed. He was practically yelling into the phone at this point. "Damn! Damn! Damn!" Cash mumbled while beating his hand on the steering wheel. "Thanks baby girl! I'll be by there later to do what we do," he said damn near sobbing.

Hanging up the phone Cash couldn't believe what had just been revealed to him. Silk was looking at Cash wondering what could've broken his spirits so abruptly.

"What's good?" Silk questioned.

Cash had fear written all over his face. Cash said, "We done fucked all the way up dawg!!"

"Wha..., wha..., what... the fuck you mean?" Silk stammered.

"We didn't kill King," Cash whispered. "We didn't kill King!! We didn't kill King," Cash kept repeating, not understanding.

"Then who did we kill?" Silk asked shocked at hearing the news. "Who was driving the car?? He asked as questions formulated in his mind.

Cash just sat there, replaying the events from that night. All he could see was the black Lac with tinted windows. He assumed it was King driving because that was his car. It never crossed his mind that someone besides King would be driving the car.

"Damn," was all he could say at the moment. "Candy!"

Hearing her name, Silk registered what they had done and all the air seem to leave his body as he struggled to breathe.

That night they both had seen the news about a woman possibly being dead from a car crash. The reporter never mention that the woman had been shot. It was just reported that the woman had been found in a car after it veered off the road. Cash, nor Silk ever heard King's name mentioned so they assumed they had gotten their man.

"Suck that dick!" King said, ramming his dick in and out of her mouth viciously while Twan fucked her in the ass.

"Hmmm....hmmmm...." Kiki tried moaning with dick in her mouth as Twan was dogging her like the whore that she was.

"Damn, I'm bouta nut in yo mouth bitch!" King said fucking her mouth.

Twan exploded in her ass just as the words left King's mouth. "Agh! Aghhh! Oh shit!" Twan yelled, grabbing her by the waist forcefully. He pulled out of her ass and sprayed come all over her ass cheeks. Twan backed up and went into the bathroom to clean himself up, while King finished his business.

"Turn around," King instructed her. When she turned around King shoved his dick right into her pussy. Her pussy was so tight and warm it put him in a trance. He grabbed her hips and dug his nails into her waist viciously. He was hurting her so bad she tried to get away. He was holding on for dear life.

"Ow! Ow! King stop!" She demanded. "Ow shit! Please King you're hurting me," Kiki pleaded as tears ran down her face.

"I'm bout to bust, come here!! Oh! Shittt! Come here!!"

Glad to hear him say that, she turned around and got on her knees for him to shoot in her mouth. When she looked up, she saw the devil on his face. King deep stroked her mouth with no remorse as she gagged. His semen was all in her mouth, causing her to almost throw up. When he finally pulled his cock out of her mouth, he was exhausted.

Kiki got up feeling like a crackhead after what they had done to her. They promised her that if she gave them info on Cash, they would give her $100,000 and fuck her like she ain't never been fucked. They promised to also give her 4 1/2 ounces of cocaine.

As everybody got themselves together, King sat in a chair waiting on Kiki to come out of the bathroom. When she came out of the bathroom, she sat beside King.

"Did you enjoy that?" She asked him.

"Yeah," he said as he handed her the biggest block of cocaine her eyes that ever laid eyes on.

She took the coke and said, "Thank you Daddy!!" She stood up and ran straight to the bathroom.

When the door closed Twan picked up her phone. After what had taken place, they had to kill her. There was no way she could stay alive. What would it cost for her to set them up for Cash? That's how the game goes. She had to go! They laced the Coke in the brick with straight fentanyl!! She was sure to be dead in about five minutes.

A couple minutes went by before King asked, "Do you think she's dead by now?"

"I'll go see," Twan said as he went to the bathroom. When Twan opened the door he couldn't believe what he saw.

Kiki was sitting on the toilet with thick white foam running out of her mouth, down to her chest. He backed up and turned around, King was already out the door.

Twan tucked her phone in his pocket, then walked out of the door.

EPILOGUE

Cash was online reading the newspaper articles about the incident with Candy. He was completely blindsided by the fact that she was the one driving King's car.

Knock, knock he heard on the door. "Who is it?" Cash asked as he grabbed his 40 caliber that was sitting on his lap.

"It's Dreak!"

After looking through the peep hole and feeling secure, Cash unlocked the door. He stepped aside so that Dreak good come in.

"Damn! Nigga why are you acting so paranoid and shit?" Dreak asked while smoking.

"You can never be too safe," Cash replied, looking at the door, then going back into the kitchen. "What can I do for you?"

"Shit! Let me get a baby," Dreak stated. Meaning 4 1/2 ounces of cocaine.

Cash moved around the kitchen, putting his order together as Dreak question him about the incident with Candy.

"Have you heard about the chick that got killed?"

Playing dumb he replied, "No," Just to see what Dreak's reply would be.

"Everybody thought it was a car wreck at first, then they discovered that she had been shot multiple times," he explained.

"Niggas thought it was King since it was his car that was shown at the scene."

"That's wild as fuck," Cash replied sarcastically.

"The latest shit is that King got $100,000 on the head of whoever is responsible," Dreak stated.

"Is that right?" Cash retorted, staring at him with hatred.

"Oh yeah! I wish I knew who it was so that I could get that money," Dreak confessed.

Cash couldn't get this nigga out of his presence fast enough. "$3600 nigga!" Cash said, shoving the drugs into his chest forcefully.

"What the fuck? You've been charging me $2000," Dreak whined.

"The price just went up," Cash had started feeling annoyed. "Take it! Or leave it!" He stated, pulling out his pistol.

Dreak counted out the money then dropped it on the table, not understanding what just happened. As he walked out of the house, it took everything in Cash to not blow his head off. He locked the door, then grab the money off the table as his phone rang again.

Cash answered without looking to see who the caller was, but the phone hung up. When he looked at the number, he noticed it was Kiki. He started fucking with the cocaine on the table, as a chirp came through, indicating he had a message.

"What's good Daddy?" The text read.

He replied, "Shit! Bouta come over there so you can swallow this dick."

Instantly she replied back. "OK! The door will be open. I'm about to jump into the shower."

"Fuck it!" Cash mumbled. All work and no play is bad for your health. Grabbing his car keys and pistol, Cash exited the house to go to Kiki's.

"Yo! Can you believe this trick ass nigga just took the bait?" King asked in disbelief.

"Hell naw!" Twan replied, laughing hysterically.

"Damn, that bitch starting to stink like hell," King grabbed his nose, referring to Kiki's dead body that's been sitting in the house all day.

"He gonna smell that shit as soon as he walks in," Twan suggested.

"Man that nigga gonna be thinking about getting his dick wet. The smell will be the last thing on his mind," King stated while blowing a thick cloud of Hydro smoke.

It had been almost twenty minutes since he last text Cash. "What's taking this nigga so long?" King asked, getting impatient.

"Oh shit! I see some headlights turning into the driveway!" Twan yelled.

"Get ready! It's going to be him," King said sliding into the closet.

Thump! Thump!

"Twan you hear that shit?" King asked.

"He gotta have somebody with him, I heard two doors close."

'I'd rather be a NIGGA. So we can get drunk and smoke weed all day.' 2Pac could be hard playing when Cash waltzed in. That was him and Kiki's song that they smoked too!

"Damn, she's smoking some pressure," Silk said coming in behind Cash.

"Kiki!!! Kiki!!!" Cash yelled. "Lock the door nigga," he told silk as he walked towards the back room. Cash move towards the bedroom with Silk on his heels. Neither one of them heard Twan getting out of the closet as they walked into the bathroom where the music was coming from.

Cash started sniffing the air suspiciously. "Yo! What the fuck is that?" He asked.

Silk's mind was on tricking, so nothing else was important at the time. "Yeah! I smell some gas and I'm ready to hit some ass," Silk replied, jokingly.

Cash pulled his gun out and took the safety off to be ready just in case need be. Yanking the bathroom door open, then seeing the tub empty, threw him off. Kiki's phone was on the back of the toilet, 2Pac was still rapping as Cash got a feeling that something was definitely wrong.

When he turned around, Silk was standing there with the crazy look on his face. Cash moved towards the bedroom and as he got closer the smell got stronger.

"I smell that shit now," Silk said on the verge of vomiting.

Just as Cash was about to open the door he heard a bullet being chambered, chik! Chik! He turned, thinking it was Silk finally getting focused on the situation at hand. What he saw couldn't have been real, or so he thought!

Twan stood behind, with a big ass P 89 pointed at his head. His thoughts were everywhere at that moment.

"Drop the gun nigga," Twan said shoving the gun in the back of Silk's head.

Before Twan could ask again, King came out of the bedroom. Off instincts, Cash started busting at King! Fow! Fow! Fow! With no choice, but to kill or be killed!

Twan blew Silk's thoughts out of his face.

Boom!

Blood splattered all over Cash as he fired at King.

King was returning fire at the same time. Whoom! Whoom!

Twan then took cover behind the wall. Cash had backed all the way out the front door and fell. Fow! Fow!

Cash took several shots to the chest.

"Yo! King!" Twan yelled. "King!" There was no reply. Twan had seen King fire at Cash as he back pedaled. As Cash got up to reach for the door handle, he heard Twan calling King. Twan couldn't fathom the thought of letting King's killer go scott free. He jumped up from behind the wall and started busting at Cash!

He ran out the house shooting while trying to hit anything. Cash had already been hit in his back while flying. Boom! Boom! Boom he shot back recklessly! His reckless shooting had paid off as he fired four shots. Fiy! Fiy! Fiy! Fiy! Two of the shots found it's mark in Twan's face, killing him instantly.

The shots Cash had taken threw him out the front door onto the lawn. He managed to go to his car after killing Twan and driving away, hurt badly.

King heard the commotion taking place while he was slumped in the back room. That's when flashbacks were running through his mind of his life. Images of Candy, his father and Sam playing basketball were like a film reel. Candy's voice echoed in his mind, telling him he still had things to take care of, giving him strength.

Somehow he mustered up enough strength to stand up. He staggered into the hallway and noticed a pair of legs laying there. With bleeding coming out of his mouth and his gun raised, he continued up the hallway. Once he got to the corner, he kicked the victim that was laying there. He kicked him repeatedly, looking for a response. There was none. Nobody moved.

When he moved towards the front door, what he saw devastated him. Twan was there, sprawled out in a puddle of blood, with a gaping hole in the back of his head. King threw up instantly! His brother, his best friend was gone and there was nothing he could do for him.

Not five feet from Twan lay Silk. He was missing his whole face, guaranteeing that he was gonna have a funeral with a closed casket.

King could feel his own life slipping away from him with each passing second. He stumbled out the front door and continued around the corner. Luckily for him, it was dark and they were in the projects. *"If I can only make it to my car,"* King thought.

When he saw his car, he was exhausted but relieved at the same time. He finally got to his car and open the door. Using what energy he had left, he climbed in and tried to crank it up. He didn't have the strength to do anything else.

He sat there, slumped in his car, waiting on death to come and get him. Thoughts of being with his mom and Candy consumed him.

"Oh! Shit!! King is that you?" A female's voice asked.

King used the last remaining strength he had to raise his gun. After that he surrendered to total blackness as it engulfed him.

To be continued!!

David Simpson was born and raised in Salisbury, NC. He lost both his parents at a young age. David grew up playing basketball and eventually decided to play in the other game as well.

He has taken loses as well as gains and he decided, during his last federal bid, to make a better way of living. He can still hustle, he just changed the hustle.

While at US Penitentiary Hazleton, he wrote faithfully. He would like to thank all his readers in advance and promises to keep dropping fiya.

He enjoys playing basketball, writing, and spending time with his kids.